MARRIAGE OF A THOUSAND LIES

MARRIAGE OF A THOUSAND LIES

SJ Sindu

Published by
Soho Press, Inc.
853 Broadway
New York, NY 10003

Library of Congress Cataloging-in-Publication Data
Sindu, SJ.
Marriage of a thousand lies / SJ Sindu.

ISBN 978-1-61695-790-2
eISBN 978-1-61695-791-9

1. Lesbians—Fiction. 2. Marriage—Fiction. 3. Sri Lankans—United
States—Fiction. 4. Immigrant families—Fiction. 5. Choice
(Psychology)—Fiction. 6. Psychological fiction. I. Title
PS3619.I5688 M37 2017 813'.6—dc23 2016047187

Printed in the United States of America

10 9 8 7 6 5 4 3 2 1

For all my families—blood, chosen, desi, queer—

MARRIAGE OF A THOUSAND LIES

When I was nine I wanted a short-sleeved button-down shirt. Amma refused to buy one from the boys' section, pushed me instead toward the pinks and butterflies in the girls', so I told her I needed one for a school play. I wore it open when I biked down hills, the wind slipping its fingers through the loose weave, cooling my sweat through my tank top. My best friend Nisha told me I'd make a cute boy, and her words squeezed something deep inside my bones, pried loose the skin between my legs. Pin pricks. Needles. My first lie.

THE GAME

Music pumps from the walls and jumps off the tin roof tiles. Gay night at the local dive, and it's a clash of rainbow shirts against walls of dusty license plates. College lesbians and blue-collar queers slide around each other in the hot, coffin-shaped bar. Hands slip numbers over sticky tables, roaming thumbs hook over edges of rough denim, drunken tongues on beads of sweat, lips mix over whispered lies, skin on skin without room for truths and this is why we're here.

"Two o'clock," Kris says. "Don't look." He leans my way over a tall, spindly table and sips his long island iced tea through a stirrer held between his teeth. His hair, which he grows out into a swoop over his left eye, falls down between us like a curtain. We've both taken off our wedding rings. Mine rests in a tiny glass tray in our bathroom. Kris's is placed carefully on his nightstand next to his multivitamins.

The walls vibrate with the bass, bouncing across my skin. I drink my beer and check my phone, wondering if it's my ex calling, but it's only my mother.

"Your two o'clock, or mine?" I say.

"Mine." Kris shakes the hair out of his eyes and points at my phone. "Is it Emily?"

"No." I put my phone back in my pocket. It's only been a couple of weeks since Emily and I broke up, but the time has stretched me out. My insides feel ragged and thin. I want the dance floor to swell up with people, the music to climb inside me and wipe my brain clean.

Kris stares hard at his glass, now mostly filled with ice, the dark tea slurped down to the last inch. Even at twenty-seven, he is still all angles that push at his clothing.

I drain the last of my beer and walk toward the bar. Kris's two o'clock is a man sitting at the table next to ours in a Red Sox hat and a white Hanes shirt. He holds his Bud Light to his lips but doesn't drink.

I walk up next to a woman on a bar stool whose sad eyes droop down at the outer corners like they're going to tip the pupils right out of her face. My phone buzzes. I ignore it. The woman smiles at me, her mouth edged in red lipstick. I could take her into a bathroom stall and push her up against the cold brick walls. I think of that red, red mouth gaping open, lipstick smeared, fingers clutching at me, lips slippery on my fingers and mouth.

I smile back. She slides her bar stool closer and touches my arm when she talks, her fingers tingling the skin where I've pushed up the sleeves of my button-down. Kris would say it was worth it. A fuck's a fuck, he would say.

My phone buzzes. Amma again. I leave the woman smiling and walk back to where Kris is standing, stirring the ice in his glass around and around. This is the first time we've gone out in months—my unemployment and his busy work schedule as a second-pass message editor for a greeting card company keeps us out of the bars and at home doing normal married people things like Amma always wanted. Kris spends his nights trying to write his own greetings and staring at the cards framed over his desk, the few he got published when he first left engineering and started in this business. I spend my nights drawing commissions for horny suburban fanboys with money to waste—too-thin elves facing off against tentacled monsters, custom Sailor Scouts, coy anime girls frolicking at the beach, well-endowed geishas undressing in dimly-lit rooms.

"So?" Kris says. He tips his glass back and shakes an ice cube into his mouth.

"The one at the bar? I don't think so."

"A fuck's a fuck." He holds the ice cube between his teeth and talks around it. "Emily's getting laid. Why shouldn't you?"

"Shut up." I wish I had bought another beer so that I'd have something to hold onto, so that the cold of it could take my mind off the ache in my stomach. My hands grasp at the air.

The man in the Red Sox hat stares hard at Kris through the darkness of the bar.

"Emily was no Nisha," Kris says. He raises his empty glass. "To Nisha, your oldest and truest."

I feel the outline of my phone through my pocket and think about calling Nisha.

"Red Sox Hat seems interested," I say.

"He's drinking a Bud Light."

"A fuck's a fuck."

I haven't spoken to Nisha since my wedding, haven't had a meaningful conversation with her since we graduated from high school four years before that. I tap my fingers on the table. What would she say if I called her now?

"He's not bad looking." Kris tucks a piece of hair behind his ear and looks again at the man, letting his gaze linger. He crunches down on another ice cube. "He's coming over."

Red Sox Hat puts his enormous biceps on our table, which creaks under the pressure. He's younger-looking close up, probably still in his early twenties, still in college. Kris sits up a bit straighter.

The man smirks at me and says, "Can I buy you a drink?"

Before I can react, Kris reaches across the table and folds his fingers over my wrist. My phone buzzes.

"This one's mine," Kris says.

Red Sox Hat gets up off the table and looks from Kris to me and back to Kris. "My mistake." He walks back to his table.

I wrench myself from Kris's grip. He puts his forehead in his hands.

"Sorry," I say. "I thought he was looking at you."

Kris nods to the table. I rub my wrist where he held it. We have an agreement that he'll intervene if guys hit on me, but he overdoes it.

"I knew these boots were a bad idea," I say. Kris had picked them out. "I look straight."

"How's this for a greeting? Roses are red, violets are blue."

"Is now really the time?"

"Every guy I like just wants to sleep with you."

"Wonderful. You should write greetings for a living."

Kris lifts his head up and catches my eye. We laugh at the same time. Our heads tip toward each other and we clutch the table for support. Some of the thinness inside me fades. I feel almost solid.

Back in our two-story cape outside of Bridgeport, Kris and I run on autopilot like we do every night when neither of us is getting laid. I track down one of our favorite Indian movies in a stack of DVDs on top of the TV, the cases lost or in storage or thrown accidentally into the recycling. Kris noisily makes Maggi noodles on the stove. We act against a backdrop of crawling-orchid wallpaper with curtains and light switch plates that match seamlessly. The talk of painting when we first moved in gave way to an affectionate tolerance for the pantheon of flowers that fly awkwardly across the walls, the permanently clogged fireplace, and the bathroom where every surface is mirrored—Kris's favorite place to shower with his rotating collection of boyfriends and hookups.

We settle down in the dark with our steaming bowls of Maggi. Kris leans his head on my shoulder and we watch Kajol, the heroine, run around somewhere in Europe—snowcapped mountains behind her—while wind rips through her saree and scatters it behind her like a flag. The whole song sequence is a dream in the hero's mind as he stares at the full moon and strums his cittern, depressed that the girl he loves is getting an arranged marriage. His balding father sits down beside him, squints at the moon, and tells him to go after her. "The bride belongs to the man who brings her home," he says.

Kris's phone rings.

"It's Laila Aunty," he says, handing it to me.

I pause the movie and get up from the couch. Laila Aunty is the woman that my father married after he left Amma. I can never talk to her sitting down. Her voice on the phone is hushed in a tone she hasn't used since my second-oldest sister Vidya ran away with a black man from Kentucky.

"Lakshmi," she says. "You are home, no?" Laila Aunty adds "no" to the end of all her sentences—residue from her British schooling.

I hate her voice.

"I'm home," I say. I walk into the kitchen. My feet slip with sweat.

"You should call more."

I've never called her. If I feel the need to hear Appa's voice, I call his cell directly.

"I've meant to call," I say. "I've just been very busy." I wipe my hands on a dishrag and throw away a condom wrapper that was on the counter next to the microwave. I feel naked, like she can see through me and into the house, like she's judging the piles of dishes that only get done when Kris puts on his big yellow gloves and sanitizes them all with scalding water because he doesn't believe dishwashers can do the job right. My empty beer bottles stand in clusters on the kitchen table. Recycling spills from the corner trashcan. Laila Aunty would faint if she could see it.

Laila Aunty coughs. "I have some bad news, Lucky."

I pick up a cup that may have once held tomato juice. It slips and lands with a thud against the stainless-steel sink.

"Your grandmother is in the hospital. You need to come home, no?"

I drive to Boston that night. I miss the city. Muggy air billows from the mountains and seeps into the car. Dingy clouds hang too low over dry patches of grass. Masspike plays hide and seek around tufted green hills. I always forget how narrow the streets are in the old towns just north of Boston, how you can almost stick your hand out of the car window and ruffle the next driver's hair. Speeding in Winchester feels like scraping the edge of a cliff, moment after moment of narrow escapes and near disasters, chasing the turn of the road, inches away from being swallowed by the night and not caring one bit, one flick of the wheel on Arlington Road and a cold lake awaits, who do I have to live for, a crash bang and blackness, a final note that sounds oh so good and true.

Amma's house sits at the end of Emerson Drive in Winchester—the house my parents bought before Appa got tenure at Northeastern, before Amma finished her dentistry certification—a tiny cape house with powder-green paint peeling off the siding, nestled in between other hundred-year-old houses with damp, unfinished basements that flood every spring with the river. This block is the cheapest in town.

Through the lit window, I see Amma sitting in the kitchen waiting for me. Laila Aunty and Appa are there, too, milling around our old house like flies. Amma has her face in her hands. She puts her elbows on the blue Formica kitchen island, wearing one of her usual cotton nightgowns that button all the way down over her thick body. Her frizzy gray hair is pulled back from her face.

I enter with my key. Everyone turns toward the door but no one moves.

Appa's thinning hair is dyed black, his skin leathery from

his youth in Sri Lanka, dark and tough. He stands at the bottom of the stairs with his hands in the pockets of his pleated khakis, wearing a blue sports coat that's starting to rub down to periwinkle at the elbows. Beside the faded orange walls of our kitchen, he seems softened, not diminished but simply worn around the edges like an old photograph. A thin scar snakes down his cheek. When I was little, I liked to trace its raised ridge with my finger and ask how he got it. The story changed every time.

"You cut your hair again," he says.

He says it every time he sees me, though I've had it short for years. He clears his throat. He's picked up smoking again.

Laila Aunty eyes the two of us before she laughs—a high, tittering giggle that sets my teeth on edge—and comes to hug me. Her hair, as usual, is plaited modestly at the back. Her heavy gold earrings scratch my face when she pulls me close to her sandalwood scent.

I stand there until she stops.

"You're too thin, dear," she says. "But beautiful as always, no." She pushes my bangs out of my eyes and rubs my cheek while I try not to pull away.

Amma clears her throat. Laila Aunty shrinks back.

Amma's hug smells like vanilla-cake shampoo. Every year for her birthday, my sister Vidya sends this shampoo to Amma, no return address. And even though Amma pretends to throw it out, pretends that she's too proud to accept something from her wayward, estranged daughter, we all know she fishes it out of the trash once everyone leaves, and uses it religiously until it runs out.

Amma sits me down on one of the three stools at the kitchen

island. Three is a strange number, and we always used to have someone standing during family meals, but the stools all match so Amma never wanted to buy a fourth one. She starts to make tea on the stove.

"I can do that," I say, getting up from the stool.

She waves her hand. "No, no. Your tea is terrible."

I sit back down and wait for her to tell me about Grandmother. The news comes in little spurts. Amma speaks to the pot in which she boils the tea, and later to the cups as she stirs in the sugar.

"She fell down the stairs. She's getting so old, you know." Amma pauses with the clink clink of the sugar spoon against the ceramic cups. "We went to the hospital." Clink clink. "She's fine, upstairs resting."

Laila Aunty studies the picture wall of my family's frozen smiles. She stands for a long time in front of my oldest sister Shyama's wooden plaques from high school: 4.0 GPA, National Merit, National Honor Society, Honor Roll all four years; framed pictures of Shyama graduating cum laude from Columbia, getting married, receiving her Master's from NYU, holding her newborn son.

Pictures of my second-oldest sister Vidya stop around the time she graduated from college. She wears tight clothes in her high school pictures, the prettiest one of all of us with her curls and Bollywood features, posing next to her sculptures and paintings.

Photos of me are all braces and thick glasses, knobby knees and too-sharp elbows, except for the one of me in my Bharatanatyam dancing costume, shining with gold thread and jewelry surrounded by a gilded frame, giant, almost life-size.

It's the one picture where I don't look awkward or gangly. I'm svelte, feminine, almost sexy, silk pleats pooling between my legs, my body in an impossible pose of movement. The dancer, the black sheep, fucked from birth, but the me in the pictures didn't know it then.

Amma puts a steaming cup of tea in front of me. My glasses fog up. I wrap my hands around the cup and soak the warmth into my skin.

"This was a close call." Amma takes her own cup of tea in a chipped mug that says "#1 Dad," and takes a sip.

Appa picks up the two other cups and gives one to Laila Aunty. They get tea in delicate flower-printed teacups, which Amma reserves for guests who aren't family. Laila Aunty goes back to studying the photo wall.

Appa rubs nervously at his mustache, which he's forgotten to dye black. "It would be nice if you stayed with your mother for a while, Lucky. She needs the help." He clears his throat and brushes down his mustache. He rocks back and forth on the balls of his feet, something he does when he's ready to leave a place.

Laila Aunty pretends not to notice. Instead she stares at a picture of my wedding, Kris and me looking like we're about to start laughing—Kris in his white and gold turban, me dolled up in a thick red saree, us looking at each other, sharing what my mother thinks is a moment of love. My thali, the thick gold chain that Kris tied around my neck to signify our marriage, glints in the photo. The light of the flash reflects off the thali and onto our skins. Laila Aunty tips back her teacup and drinks fast, her neck ballooning out every time she swallows. The silence gets thirsty, settles on our shoulders like a winter coat.

Let me tell you something about being brown like me: your story is already written for you. Your free will, your love, your failure, all of it scratched into the cosmos before you're even born. My mother calls it fate, the story written on your head by the stars, by the gods, never by you.

Everyone is watching you, all the time, praising you when you abide by your directives, waiting until you screw up. And you will screw up.

I coasted by for longer than most people. Most stray early, dating in high school or wearing the wrong clothes, maybe piercing something they shouldn't, drinking like hell in college. But then they shape up, put on a suit and go to their big-kid jobs in the swanky part of town, play middle management at biotech and engineering firms, or go to med school. They get married to other brown people and pop out some brown kids, buy a nice cookie-cutter house and everything is forgiven. As long as you follow your directives in the end, no matter how many lies you have to tell. But here's the truth: I'm still lying.

When Appa and Laila Aunty finally leave, Amma washes their teacups by hand and puts them away in the cabinet that needs a fresh coat of paint.

I walk up the navy-carpeted stairs to my old bedroom where Grandmother now sleeps. It's a long, narrow blue box with two gable windows that cut through the slanted roof. My old computer, the bookshelves that used to hold my textbooks, they're all still there, resting heavily against the walls. Even my wrought-iron bed that's gritty from too much dust. And if I squint through the darkness, my sister Vidya's high school final art project—a metal sculpture painted bright orange—sits where it always has on the window ledge.

I can just make out a mound under the blankets, rising and falling with Grandmother's breath. I watch until my breath matches hers, then sneak back downstairs to help Amma wipe down the kitchen counters before bed. The carpet soaks up my footfalls like sand.

Grandmother gets up early the next morning. By the time I come downstairs, she's sitting on a folding chair in the living room, watching a Tamil news show about the American election. On the screen, Obama smiles and gives a speech about healthcare reform while Tamil subtitles scroll underneath his face. Grandmother hunches from age, her skin melted into many little wrinkles. Her smile reveals three missing front teeth—one more than the last time I saw her—and a mouth permanently stained red from chewing betel leaves.

She was a beauty in her day. The very few photos she had taken—one of her marriage and one of her graduation—show a smooth-skinned, round-faced girl with pearls laced through her bun. She wears a grand saree and smiles coyly into the camera. When I was little, I thought she was some kind of heiress. She laughed and set me straight. "Those are plastic beads in my hair," she said. "And that's a simple cotton saree." For weeks I stared at the photo, wondering how the camera could transform a working-class girl into a princess on the page.

I bend down and she kisses me with one long sniff on each cheek. She smells like baby powder and betel juice. I sink into the couch and check my phone. Still no contact from Emily. Already my insides feel fuller, some of the thinness filled in by travel. Outside, through the sliding-glass doors to the water-stained deck, Amma's vegetable garden lies cushioned by the overgrown backyard. In middle school I had taken the mean notes that kids slipped into my locker and buried them under that garden, in between the neat rows of cabbages and carrots.

Grandmother tells me the plot of her favorite show, a Tamil soap opera, and I try my best to follow. My Tamil isn't the most fluent. Kris and I don't use it at home. I can understand fairly well but I have an accent when I try to speak. My stomach can't make the guttural sounds Tamil demands. My speech comes out sounding too flat, too delicate, too American. Tamil needs to be spoken deep and strong with big lungs.

"How are your studies?" Grandmother asks, switching to English.

I snap to attention.

Grandmother smiles. She was once a teacher at a Catholic school in Sri Lanka, fluent in English. Now she only uses it when she thinks I'm not listening or when she really wants me to understand.

"I'm not in school anymore, Ammamma." I tell her this every time I visit, but she forgets. "I work at a company now." I don't. I got laid off months ago. I haven't even told Amma yet.

She nods slowly—my American accent takes a while for her

to process—and squints again at the TV. Obama has stopped speaking for a biscuit commercial with a white-skinned woman and her long, straight black hair that slips across her back like water.

"Your Amma had to go to work," Grandmother says.

"How do you feel? Does it hurt?"

"I always hurt." She shakes her head when she speaks, as if she's shaking the syllables from her mouth.

"But the fall. Do you hurt from your fall?"

She looks at me, and I can see the way her eyes are fading to clear at the edges, fast losing their deep burgundy color. "Fall? I didn't fall."

Grandmother was the first in our family to benefit from Sri Lanka's free higher education system. She got a degree in English and dreamed of teaching at a private school. She married one of her university professors, seventeen years her senior, who promised to let her teach after marriage. And he did, for a year, before she got pregnant. Grandmother's first maternity leave stretched and stretched until it swallowed the rest of her life.

"She said she didn't fall," I say to Amma when she comes home from work.

Amma's face looks like a deflated balloon. She once looked like Vidya, my prettiest sister, thin and oval-faced. Now Amma is stiff with experience, her flesh choking her bones with too much skin. She purses her lips.

"She gets like that sometimes," Amma says. "Forgets things. She's getting older."

Grandmother dozes on the couch. Amma has told her she's

only allowed to climb up the stairs to go to bed at night, and down them in the mornings. We keep our voices low. Amma unpacks her lunch bag, the small container of rice and curry that she takes to work every day, an orange or banana, and a tiny portion of Greek yogurt with sugar that she claims tastes like the yogurt they made back home in Sri Lanka. Amma eats a lot of foods because they're like the ones she used to eat as a little girl. She even goes out of her way to find smaller, more tropical bananas at Stop & Shop.

I fill up the electric kettle and wait for the water to boil for Amma's after-work tea. Kris and I tried to continue high tea after we got married but it never stuck. Our tea had a weird aftertaste like plastic, too sweet, too bitter, too dark, too light with too much milk. Kris isn't a fan of the dark Ceylon tea that Amma drinks. He wants expensive tea from stores run by white hippies, stores that sell tea leaves mixed with dried herbs and fruits. I can't stand them, the teas that are too weak and not sweet enough, teas that come with their own accessories.

I check my phone for any contact from Emily. Nothing, no texts, no calls. I put the phone away.

"Can't you live without your phone?" Amma says.

I set out three mugs in a row and put a tea bag in each. When the kettle dings, I pour hissing water into the mugs. The tea bleeds into the water.

Amma washes out her lunch containers in the sink and sets them to dry on the towel that covers part of the blue Formica counter. The once-tangerine kitchen walls are faded from all of Grandmother's oily cooking.

I hold each tea bag by its string and bob it up and down in the water until the liquid is dark like oil.

"Nisha's coming by today," Amma says.

My heart speeds up at the name. I squeeze out each tea bag with a spoon and put it into the sink.

I first met Nisha in fourth grade when we moved to the same school district—me from Virginia where my sisters and I were born, Nisha from London. She had a strong English accent back then, one she lost over the years. Back then, Amma and Appa had an explosive relationship—they were either having tickling matches and cuddling on the couch, or shouting from across the room and banging doors.

"She wants to see you," Amma says.

"Great." I pour milk into one of the mugs.

Amma clucks her tongue. "Heat that up first."

"I already poured it."

"It's not tasty when you just pour it cold." She takes a glass measuring cup from the cupboard and pours more milk into it. "You can have that tea. I'll heat this up for mine and Ammamma's." She puts the measuring cup into the microwave, punches in two minutes, and sits down at the kitchen table.

I wait for the microwave, pour the newly-heated milk into the rest of the tea, and add two spoons of sugar to each cup. Grandmother is borderline diabetic but she'll be damned if she's going to drink unsweetened tea. She says the artificial sweeteners taste funny, and she always knows when we try to trick her.

Grandmother comes hobbling out of the living room to the sound of my stirring the sugar. Amma helps her climb onto one of the stools.

"You should grow out your hair, Vidya," Grandmother says.

I set the tea mug down in front of her.

"That's Lucky," Amma says. "Not Vidya."

"You made good tea, Lucky," Grandmother says, taking small sips.

⁓

Amma calls me into her room. She rummages around in her antique armoire that once belonged to Grandmother—teakwood carved with hibiscus flowers, the only inheritance Amma owns. A bookshelf next to the armoire holds Tamil romance novels on the very bottom two shelves and framed paintings of Hindu gods and goddesses on the top shelves, each painting draped with a fabric flower garland. Amma burns sandalwood incense every morning when she prays, and the smoke swirls around the room for the rest of the day, working its way into hairs and fabric, lingering like a sweet something at the backs of throats. Here's the truth: I don't believe in gods.

Amma holds out a silky beige shirt. "Wear this. You'll look nice."

The shirt shimmers through my fingers, cool to the touch. Amma waits with her hands crossed at the wrists, watching me. When I don't make a move, she walks over to me and I remember how thick she is, how she can easily block a doorway.

She pinches my bicep between two fingers.

This again.

"Your arms need to be soft, Lucky. Your arms are too hard."

I pull away. I worked for years to get my triceps to bulge.

She sits down next to me. "You need to think about the way you're looking to others." Her eyebrows make an arc across her face. She pets my hair, a shoulder-length frizz. I try hard not to flinch. "This is just too short."

"Shyama—"

"Shyama's hair is past her shoulders. You're bald!"

I scratch a place where my jeans are starting to fray.

Amma pats my hand. "You're not a child anymore, Lucky."

I concentrate on the loose thread.

"With Nisha's marriage," Amma says, "the groom's family will look at everyone around her. Even you."

The words erase my thoughts. "Nisha's getting married?"

"That's what she's coming to tell you." Amma holds out the shirt.

I take it and pull it on over my black tank top. The fabric slides cold against my skin.

"You look like a lady," Amma says. "Pretty."

In the mirror, the silk flows around my chest and the pouch of my stomach, small white flowers embroidered into the fabric. I pull at the front of it so it doesn't hug my chest.

"Stop fussing," she says.

"I look like—"

"Like a lady. You are pretty."

The word makes me squirm. Pretty is girls like Shyama who get married to the men their parents pick out, girls who never play sports or talk loudly.

Amma kisses the top of my head and smiles.

Nisha comes by for dinner, her thin torso swimming in an Indian cotton tunic. She's a good girl in the same ways that Shyama has always been a good girl. Nisha helps Amma heat up food, gets water for everyone, and makes cheerful conversation during dinner. Around her, I slouch even more than usual and forget to sit with my legs closed. Amma hisses at me to sit up straighter, to keep my knees together, to eat without spilling anything or making any noises.

"Sit up, Lucky," Amma says. "I don't know what Krishna sees in you. You're like a boy."

"Vidya's getting married," Grandmother says.

"No," Nisha says. "*I'm* getting married." She giggles and looks down at her plate. She looks like the girls in Tamil commercials—all perfect makeup and practiced allure. She has a face pinched in the center, her eyes close to a long, straight-bridged nose.

"He's a good guy," she says, and looks back down at her plate.

I don't know how she can eat with her fingers when her nails are so long and painted. She's gotten her nose pierced since the last time I saw her.

When we were young, Amma would drop me off at Nisha's house when she went to work. We played in the green space behind her apartment building, replaying scenes from our favorite Tamil movies. Nisha loved movies starring Rajnikanth, a man hero-worshipped by most Tamils. Rajnikanth would leap out of burning buildings and beat up fifty henchmen to get the girl in the end. Outside, behind the apartment building, I leapt out of cardboard boxes and climbed trees, beat up imaginary villains and saved Nisha. She pretended to wear extravagant sarees and we sang duets like they did in the movies.

After dinner, Amma and Grandmother watch Tamil game shows in the living room. Nisha and I talk in the guest bedroom. The bed sags and tips us toward each other.

"I like your shirt," Nisha says. She looks at me out of the corner of her carefully-painted eye.

I shift in my seat and press myself against the headboard. Cold permeates through my shirt. I can make out a trace of the jasmine perfume she always wears. Muffled TV music works its way through the walls.

"How's the husband?" she asks.

"How's Simmons?"

Nisha's on her third post-college program. So far she's quit pharmacy school and nursing school. Indecisive. Or just flighty.

"Boring. I hate living at home. It must be amazing to live on your own, just you and your husband. Must be romantic."

I bite down on my laugh.

She slaps my arm. "It's not funny."

The room is too hot but my fingers are freezing.

I sometimes wonder what it would've been like if we'd both come out in high school, if we would've tried dating for real. But Nisha was afraid even then. Even when we were by ourselves, she'd never acknowledge what is was that we were doing. I'd like to think that I would've come out, if she'd been willing, but that's just another lie.

Most people think the closet is a small room. They think you can touch the walls, touch the door, turn the handle, and walk free. But when you're inside it, the closet is vast. No walls, no door, just empty darkness stretching the length of the world.

Even during our on-again, off-again high school fling, Nisha never stopped pretending to like boys. She had a rotating string of boyfriends, but none that she actually seemed to like or want.

She watches the screensaver of Amma's computer and smiles with only her mouth.

I sweat cold patches into my shirt, but my skin feels too small. She stares unblinkingly at her knees. "My parents arranged this. The marriage, I mean. He's from India."

"When's the wedding?" The words feel foreign, unwieldy. My tongue can't wrap around the syllables.

"The engagement ceremony is in a few weeks." Nisha draws her knees to her chest. Her lips shimmer with a remnant of pink gloss, most of it eaten away with the meal. I try to remember what it tastes like.

"The wedding's in December," she says.

My tooth cuts skin. I lick away the blood on my lips.

This was bound to happen. Nisha's parents have been desperate to find a guy since I got married to Kris. As far as anyone knows, Kris and I fell in love.

I tried to tell Nisha once, the truth about Kris and me. It was on the morning of my wedding, and I was terrified. But Nisha refused to hear it. She kissed me on the cheek to silence me, and left the room. That was four years ago, and after that I didn't hear from her.

Nisha scoots closer and presses up against my side. I wrap my arms around her. She puts her head on my shoulder.

"Do you want this?" I ask.

She breathes in and out. I press my cheek against her head. The words sink in. Nisha is getting married. The wedding's in December. Wedding. Married. Nisha.

"Sometimes I wish you were a boy," Nisha says.

A wedding that wouldn't be a lie. A true marriage with love, and children, and nothing extra on the side. It was hard to imagine.

Here's the truth: Sometimes I wish I were a boy, too.

The three of us—Amma, Grandmother and I—prowl around the house for days like cats in a cage. We run into each other in the turns of hallways. We close doors too fast. Grandmother reminds us of the pain she's in, but denies that she fell down the stairs. A wheezing cough buds in her throat. She tells me every day to grow out my hair.

During the day while Amma's at work, I sit with Grandmother and watch her watch TV. I tell Amma I'm working from home. She believes me, and doesn't ask about the graphics tablet and pen plugged into my laptop. When I was a programmer, I worked from home most of the time. Amma doesn't know that I haven't worked for months, that my only source of employment has been drawing commissioned digital art. The gigs pay enough to shut Kris's face about contributing to the household, but I'm not artistic like my sister Vidya, who could manipulate pigments and shape stories with her hands, make scenes out of nothing. She's the real artist. I can't do what she did, but I'm good enough to bring to life the orcs and gladiators and mermaids of teenagers' dreams.

When she watches TV, Grandmother chews betel leaves with an acrid, spicy mixture that scratches the inside of my nostrils. She's done this since I was a kid visiting her in Sri Lanka.

She wraps the thick, veined leaves around red-soaked coconut gratings, softened areca nuts, slaked lime paste, and spices I can't name. After meals she chews coconut gratings that smell like perfume, mixed with candy-coated fennel seeds for fresh breath. Amma doesn't approve, always scrunches her face and turns her head, but I've always loved watching Grandmother's mouth ooze with red juice that she spits into a metal cup. The liquid clangs against the metal, her aim honed.

She let me chew after my twenty-second birthday, when she first came to live with Amma from Sri Lanka. I couldn't stomach the sharp acidic flavor that spread over my tongue. I had to run to the trashcan to spit it out. I learned instead how to fold the betel leaves, how to chop and soak the areca nuts, which mixtures went with what, what kind Grandmother liked.

Now I buy ingredients from a local Indian store and fold betel leaves for Grandmother. She tells me stories of Sri Lanka while she chews, and I listen while I draw. She tells me how she spent time in a refugee camp during the civil war, how the old woman in the tent next to hers had no arm, how the buses to Jaffna would be stopped, searched, sometimes bombed.

"We never knew what was coming." She stuffs a leaf in her mouth. Her eyes flutter closed. She bites down slowly, savoring the way the leaf bursts and fills her mouth with juices.

I draw pictures of a woman in a ratty saree, the tail of it wrapped around her arm where it ends at the elbows. I'll never be able to sell these, or show them to Amma, who would cluck her tongue and tell me I should draw pictures of nice things like flowers and beautiful girls. The woman's eyes pull with emptiness. I don't think I'll be able to sell any prints of this on my website, but I'm tired of just drawing happy anime characters and fan couples in sexy boudoir scenes. Once when I was in high school, before I started drawing for money, back when I still thought I could be a real artist, Vidya looked at my drawings and said, "Everyone you draw has sadness in their eyes."

"They're smiling," I said.

She said, "Like they're quietly burning from the inside."

"Your mother was a young woman," Grandmother says. "It was a dangerous time for young women. She wants you to have a good life. She wants you to make all the right decisions." When she talks I can see red teeth and gums.

I shade the eyes of the woman I've drawn, hoping I can fill the emptiness in.

For as long as I've known her, Grandmother has had a routine of waking up before anyone else and making coffee. Now that she can't get down the stairs on her own, she waits in bed for Amma to help her. Once they're in the kitchen, she directs Amma on how to properly make coffee. They fight.

I avoid it all by sleeping in until after Amma goes to work. By the time I come down to microwave my coffee, Grandmother is already a few episodes deep into her Tamil soap operas. She fills me in on the latest plot developments. She asks if I'm doing well in school.

After a few days the sound of the soap operas gets to me. The dramatic music, the women's shrill fighting, the men's boasting. I understand enough Tamil to know the gist of what's happening, and a few days of angelic mothers and evil, plotting daughters is all I can take.

"Why don't we take a walk?" I open the sliding glass doors to the deck. "It's nice out."

Grandmother gets up from her folding chair and walks out onto the deck. I go to get her a light jacket and shoes. When I return, she has dragged her folding chair onto the rotting floorboards and is sitting there, watching Amma's vegetable patch.

She motions me closer. I step out onto the deck with bare feet, the cold of the wood shocking me all the way up to my knees. There's a bite to the air. I can smell the leaves starting to rot off the trees, drying and curling their tips in on themselves.

I help Grandmother pull on the jacket and wool socks with her plastic flip-flops. The breeze lifts and cools the hair on my arms.

"Why are you sitting out here?"

She holds a finger to her shrunken lips and cups her other hand around her ear.

"Do you hear that, Vidya?" she asks in Tamil.

"I'm Lucky."

"Listen."

I wait and listen, trying to hear anything more than the raccoons puttering around under the deck.

"Can you hear? Use your ears."

I listen again in the cold, with the wind that smells like trees. And then—floating on the air, a frail wailing, thin and lonesome.

"It's a baby," Grandmother says. "You're going to have a baby soon." She smiles and closes her eyes, still cupping her ear to take in the cry.

I step back, away from her, away from the deck and the cool wood under my feet.

I don't tell Amma, but every day after that when I come down for coffee, Grandmother is sitting out there on the deck, straining with her whole self to hear that sound.

Most days Nisha drops by for lunch or dinner. Her visits are long and full of complaints about her impending engagement. Except for my wedding day, Nisha and I haven't been close in a long time, but here we are, acting like best friends again.

"He's thirty-five," she tells me once. We're sitting outside on the deck to escape the heat in the house from unseasonably warm weather and Amma's hit-or-miss window air conditioners.

Nisha leans back so I can sketch her outline for a commission of a scantily clad young pixie sitting on a mushroom top in the forest.

"An engineer," she says. She curls up her nose at the word.

I draw the curve of her back. One fluid line. The pixie I'm drawing is thin and slight like Nisha, draped only in strips of fabric that move with their own wind. In her hand she holds a birdcage from which fireflies escape in an upward swirl.

"I can't believe you're still drawing," she says. "I saw your website."

My pencil stalls in the middle of a strand of hair.

"I like what you do," she says.

"It's just for money." I charge fifty dollars per hour for each commission, which is relatively high and only possible because I've been doing it for six years and have a faithful online following. Fifty dollars an hour and you get high-resolution digital art of anything you want and a frameable print.

I start drawing again, stretching the hair out in movement, and say, "It's not real art."

"I can't draw like that," Nisha says. She slides closer and puts a hand on my knee. Her fingers find a hole in my jeans. She rubs my skin with her fingernail. My stomach clenches tight.

The first time something happened between us, we were both in middle school. I'd found a bunch of mean letters from Nisha's more popular friends who didn't like us hanging out, stuffed into my locker, letters full of words like *dyke* and *transvestite*. Nisha and I burned the letters and buried the ashes in Amma's vegetable garden. Nisha held me while I cried. Maybe she recognized her friends' handwriting. Maybe she was moved by my crying. Whatever it was, something made her push my bangs out of my eyes and kiss me.

"Will you come to the engagement?" she asks.

I shade in the muscles of the pixie's leg. I'll have to darken it later. "Why wouldn't I?"

"You're going back to your husband."

"I'll be here for a while."

She scrapes at the bumps of dry skin on my knee and draws a line up my thigh with her finger. "Do you feel stuck?" she asks. "I don't want to get stuck."

"You don't have to do this, you know." I know her parents. They wouldn't force her.

I draw curls that blow back in an invisible breeze.

"I want to come home to someone," she says. Her fingers slip back and forth across my thigh. "I want to be married."

⌒

On another visit, she brings me a picture. A dark man in a suit stands next to a bright new staircase. She tells me his name is Deepak. He looks filled up with air, his smile stiff and small as if a bigger one would deflate him.

Nisha's face flushes purple. She only lets me look for a couple of seconds before she snatches it back and stuffs it in her purse.

"Well?" she says.

"He seems nice."

Her carefully-arched eyebrows sink into each other.

"Do you want me to say he's ugly?" I ask.

"He's not ugly."

She's baiting me. She wants to lash out at someone. Like it's my fault she's engaged.

"What do you want?" I say.

Part of me wants to ask her if she'd be happier if she came out. I know she wouldn't be. Last time I tried to come out, I ended up homeless and alone.

She slumps over. I snake my arm around her waist. Her weight is heavy on my side.

⌒

Nisha wants to visit our high school as a last look at her old life. Or so she says. The school's closed for summer renovations.

I haven't set foot in it for years, not even for my high school reunion.

We take the same path we used to take as teenagers. Nisha hooks her arm into my elbow and walks in step with me. Leaves blaze in the trees. My feet still know the way.

The building looks like I remember. Renovations haven't started. The mural of the school mascot—a Native American chief—is still emblazoned on the side of the brick building. When we were in school, students and teachers staged a massive walkout to change the name of the teams from the Winchester Sachems. Nisha didn't participate because her math teacher had threatened to flunk anyone who left the building.

Nisha tries the front door. Locked. We circle the building until we find an unlocked door in the back, the door that kids used to smoke outside of during lunch. The hallway provided a little niche for them to hide while they passed around their cigarettes and lighters, hand-rolled joints if they felt adventurous. I wasn't a part of that crowd, but Nisha was. She'd come back with her eyes shining. Rebellion woke something in her. Her smile would tip on the edge of wildness. She'd smell like smoke all day, right up until she washed it out of her hair in the sink before we walked home.

She holds the door open. Her eyes have that wildness.

We walk through the front hallway, looking up by habit. Every year's art students add self-portraits to a collage of ceiling tiles. My portrait is squashed up next to the men's bathroom. My skin is painted too dark, my mouth too lopsided, my eyes too flat.

A janitor in overalls watches us silently as we pass. We go upstairs to the science hallway where our class set chickens loose as a senior prank. The hallway is dark and empty. Nisha stops walking. Wooden blinds slice the light that falls onto the vinyl. I can't really see her, but there's something about the way she stands that makes me stop moving. The hallway smells like textbooks and chalk.

"I don't want to get married," she says into the empty air.

I say nothing.

"I wish I had a boyfriend," she says.

The thick air presses at my skin.

She jolts into movement and leads me to the light of the hallway, downstairs toward E wing where shop courses are held. Silence stretches out behind us. She walks me into the gym, veers left and holds open a door. I enter onto a concrete staircase.

Everything goes black when she shuts the door. I know the staircase leads to the wrestling room. Wall-to-wall padding reaching up to the ceiling. Gym teachers used it for the yoga unit.

Our steps echo against the concrete. The blackness is all encompassing, thick and impenetrable except for a hole in the ceiling that lets in a thin beam of light. I can make out the dim outlines of the room. The sweat of many wrestling practices floats out of the red mats. Nisha puts a hand in the middle of my back and pushes me into the room.

"I don't want to get married," she says again. She slides down the padded blue walls.

I kneel in front of her. "You don't have to get married."

"Oh, don't be silly. Of course I do. But I don't *want* to. Does that make sense?"

"No." I try to smile but my face won't move.

"I want to get married. Just not like this."

"Like what?"

"I want to—you know, I want to date."

She grips my arm. Tight.

"You don't understand, Lucky."

She turns my face toward her. Her fingers press hard against my skin. She moves closer. The mats squeak. I can almost see the pinprick of light reflected in her eyes. Veins pump in my skull.

"I'm married," I say.

With a strength I couldn't have imagined coming out of her thin frame, she pushes me down onto the mat. She hovers over me. I can only see her outline. She pulls off her dress in one fluid motion.

"What do you want me to do?" I say.

Her outline swallows up my vision. I can smell the dryness in my mouth. The air turns hot and sticky. Nisha is thin skin underneath me, salty everywhere with little black hairs that tickle my nose. We have to peel ourselves from the vinyl mats to move. I press my face against her jasmine scent and push my fingers into her. She trembles. Her nails clutch at me. The room fills up with her soft moans that come out like sighs. She whispers in my ear like a secret. Yes. Yes. I want this. Yes.

I was born bone heavy, my marrow dense like stone, calcium fibers spun tight and thick. People say that I shuffle when I walk but I know I danced beautifully. The pads of my feet are thick from carrying around the heaviness, and they let me slap the ground hard to the rhythm of the drums. I learned early on that I could thrive on the pressure in my heels. Dancing saved me.

Every summer in high school, Nisha and I danced Bharatanatyam together. We trained intensely for performances all around Boston—Indian cultural festivals, multicultural school nights, Sri Lankan community events. Most of the girls who danced with us did it because their parents made them. Their bodies refused to bend, their gestures awkward, stiff, frequently offbeat. Nisha and I danced because we wanted to. We isolated muscle groups and trained each part of ourselves to move independently. The head separate from the neck. The chest separate from the stomach. The hips separate from the torso. I was good, but Nisha was better.

Our performances used to be the only time I wore makeup and noticeable jewelry. Now when I put on makeup, I remember Nisha bending close to my face, my chin in her hands, lining my eyes with kohl, and how, when I blinked too much, she would kiss my eyebrow to distract me from the scratching of the pencil on skin.

Nisha's parents throw a party before her engagement ceremony. I spend an hour in front of the mirror, lining and relining my eyes, trying to get the color to flick up at the outer corners like Nisha always did.

Amma insists that I wear a saree, but not the navy one that I pick out.

"It's too dark, Lucky. It's not a funeral. Wear your pink one."

"Why can't you go instead?" I say.

Amma clucks her tongue. "Nisha asked you to come. Be a good friend. Sometimes I don't know what's happening to you."

Kris arrives at Amma's house two hours before the party. Amma fusses over him, over his long hair and thin frame. Oh, look at the poor husband, starving to death because his wife isn't at home to cook.

We get dressed in the guest bedroom and fight over the one small mirror on the dresser.

"What do you think?" Kris spins around. His dark Wranglers cling to his legs. He holds up a lime-green plaid tie in front of his striped shirt. "Too much?"

"Too much."

He throws the tie onto the bed and watches me get dressed. My saree glitters like shards of glass in the sun, six yards of transparent pink shot through with stones. Wrap around once and tuck. Twice around, and over the shoulder. Pleat the extra and tuck. Kris adjusts my pleats so that they ripple evenly at my feet.

On a Bharatanatyam costume, the pleats attach to the legs so that they sway with each movement, fan out and jump with the drums. When I wasn't dancing with Nisha, I watched the movement of her pleats, the starched symmetry of them, shadows flowing to the staccato beat.

I throw the extra pink material over my shoulder.

"No, no, don't do that." Kris arranges my saree so that my blouse is exposed.

I pull the blouse up. He pulls it back down.

"Kris!"

"I have a sexy wife. Let them see that." He safety-pins my saree and blouse together under my shoulder blade.

"No touching at the party," I say. I put on my thali, with its thick gold chain and two perfect circular coins flanking a Ganesh pendant. The mark of a married woman is important. Amma wouldn't let me leave the house without it. I tie a knot with the extra saree material inside my petticoat, and tuck my small flask of bourbon inside the waistband. A couple of sips at every bathroom break and I can get through this.

⌒

Kris's hand is clamped to my waist when we step up to the doorway of Nisha's parents' house. He likes to cause a stir when we walk in. Tamil couples don't often touch in public. This is Kris's way of rebelling—making them uncomfortable but staying safe, modern, and normal with a wife and a job and a house. I clench my teeth and let him hold my waist. I have to pick my battles.

The house is expansive and still crowded, shiny and new after Nisha's family remodeled it. Cherrywood floor in dizzying zig-zags, finished basement, new windows, new staircase, granite mantle, beige walls. People fill every nook, the women in sarees and jewelry that jingles when they walk, the men in sweater-vests and slacks, the kids in itchy taffeta dresses and miniature suits.

Kris drags me over to the living room where the men sit around a coffee table weighed down with Johnnie Walker bottles. They're going to stare at me. I know this, and Kris knows this, but of course he likes showing me off to the men, who find my interest in politics and business amusing. Amma's not here to tell me to go to the women. Might as well get in an argument about climate change.

The living room suffocates with the extra chairs they've squeezed in. White, wood-paneled walls bow inward toward the ceiling. The giant flat screen plays MSNBC's coverage of the Obama and Romney campaigns.

Appa's face crumples a little when he sees me. He'd rather I go to the women, too.

I sit next to Kris and arrange my saree so that my midriff doesn't show. We watch Rachel Maddow rip apart Romney's platform of trickle-down economics. Appa pours a glass of scotch for Kris and slides it to him along with a plate of hot wings. My flask lies against my belly.

Nisha sweeps into the room in the middle of low, rumbly laughter from the men. She shimmers in a lace net saree and has done up her hair in a 1960s Bollywood pouf.

"You didn't even say hi," she says to me. Her bangled hand clings to the arched doorway between the living room and the foyer. She turns and floats out of the room toward the kitchen.

I get up and follow her. The kitchen is the last place I want to be, but maybe if I put up with it, we can escape to the basement after a while. The women are all gathered around the giant kitchen island, leaning on the gleaming black granite countertops and sitting in fancy upholstered dining chairs.

" . . . and Shyama's enrolling her son in a gifted preschool next year," Laila Aunty is saying. She waves her arms around wildly like a drowning monkey. "He's so smart, you know. Just like his parents."

I try to hide behind Nisha but Laila Aunty sees me.

"Lucky, dear!" She walks out from the mass of women in the kitchen and comes toward me with her arms out wide.

I step back but she catches me. She sniffs kisses on each of my cheeks.

"You're looking so pretty," she says to the crowd. The women in the kitchen look me and Nisha up and down. "Look at you two. A pretty pair. Just like when you used to dance."

I know that on their way home, these women will talk about each other to their drunk husbands. But I can't beat my programming. In front of a crowd of brown faces, I sing and dance like a trained fucking seal.

Nisha pulls up two chairs next to each other. She sits with her ankles crossed and her hands folded in her lap. I try not to slouch or sit with my knees apart. The saree helps.

Bharatanatyam usually molds those who dance it. It leaves its mark on the dancers' bodies. They develop wrist flips and flamboyant gestures, a hip swing as they walk, a way of treading that swings their arms back and forth against their momentum. But I didn't get those marks. My muscles refused to absorb the fluid motions, the coquettish habit of making eyes bigger, the coy downward glance that Nisha did so well. Amma was always suspicious at the immutability of my body.

Laila Aunty goes on and on about how my sister Shyama's son is god's gift to earth.

"We're looking at grooming him for Exeter," she says.

The "we" is nothing more than Laila Aunty's wishful thinking. I manage to turn my snort into a cough. My sister Shyama isn't exactly fond of Laila Aunty. We all chose sides.

"Shyama's going to visit soon," Laila Aunty says. "So busy you know, with the next one on the way."

"My son just got into medical school," someone else says. "Northwestern. Best medical school, you know."

Her son and I went to the same middle school, and as I remember, he wasn't the brightest crayon in the box. But that doesn't matter, just as it doesn't matter which med school is actually highest ranked. The one her son goes to is the best. No discussion.

"I'm just glad we got a good marriage match," Nisha's mother says. She's a thin, frail woman who looks a lot like Nisha. She wears makeup and high heels, which most of the other brown women her age don't do.

"Are you excited?" someone asks Nisha.

Nisha does that shy downward glance thing. "A little."

"The poor girl is probably scared," someone else says. "Before my wedding, I thought I'd never be happy again."

"It's something quite unlike anything else, getting married. You never think you can love someone you don't even know but then you wake up one day and you do."

"Right, Lucky?"

The women laugh.

"You know," one of them says, "my husband didn't even know how to boil water when we first got married."

"We already trained our men."

"Us old women can only tell you so much about keeping a man happy these days, Nisha. I hope you're getting tips from Lucky."

None of them had advice for me when I got married. Not that I would've listened. It was Amma who gave me the talk. As she pleated my wedding saree before the ceremony, her hands stilled.

"You know how it works?" she said. "You know what happens the first time?"

I froze, not knowing the answer she wanted.

"I'll bleed," I said.

Her hand moved again, deftly folding the pleats, bangles clanging together as she worked. She pinned the pleats together and tucked them into my underskirt.

"Kris is a good boy. You got lucky."

"Amma." My head was spinning out of control. "I'm scared."

She looked at me, her eyes focusing on mine for a second before they adjusted and she was looking through me again. "You're doing the right thing," she said. "You're a normal girl. You're going to have a normal life."

In the kitchen with the gaggle of women, Nisha smiles and laughs at the appropriate times. I think about the flask resting safely inside the waistband of my saree. When the women start talking about food and swapping recipes, Nisha stands up and gives me the signal to go.

"We're going to check on the kids," she says.

"When are you going to have kids, Lucky?"

I trip over the front of my saree pleats. Nisha grabs my arm to steady me.

"I don't know if we're ready, Aunty," I say. I try to imagine Kris with a kid, holding it at arm's length because he wouldn't know what else to do with it.

"No one's ever ready. You just do it."

I follow Nisha downstairs. The basement smells like new paint. Children cluster around a projector screen in the open space of the den, the older ones playing video games while the younger ones watch with wide-open mouths. Teenagers lounge on the sectionals with their phones out.

"You haven't seen the new basement, have you," Nisha says.

She pulls me away from the kids, down the hallway to the bedrooms. She pushes me into one of the rooms and closes the door. The metallic lock clicks.

"Wait," I say. I back away.

She follows me, pinning me against the cold wall of the room. Night spills from the slit-like window above me. She slips her icy fingers underneath my saree. The moon dips everything in silver. She traces along my waist. My spine arches against her touch.

"Nisha, stop."

I catch her hand and pull it away from my skin. The place

44

where she touched me stays cold. She looks beautiful with all the makeup. Flawless, like a glass bead.

Her shimmering lips frown. "What's the problem?"

"This is your engagement party."

"I'm not engaged yet." She reaches out toward me again.

I try to slip her fingers in between mine. She snatches her hand away. Her eyebrows make one thin line across her face, dividing her skin in two. She puffs out her chest, turns, and opens the door, leaving me to watch the swish of her saree as she walks away.

I remember the flask. The metal is warm from my skin. I drink it all in one go. The bourbon scorches its way down my throat and into my limbs. I feel raw.

I wait until my heart cools, then go out to the den where the kids are playing. The teenagers get quiet when I sit on the couch. I'm too much of an adult. Married. Can't be trusted with the gossip of who-likes-whom and who-took-whom-on-a-secret-date. I don't feel like facing the women and their bullshit questions so I stay down here. I'm about to ask to play a round of Mario Kart when Laila Aunty comes downstairs to find me.

I take out my phone so I have something to hold onto.

"You should be upstairs," she says. This is one of those rare times she sounds like Amma, and I can believe she and Amma used to be best friends.

I make a show of turning off my phone. "Just checking work email, Aunty."

"Come, come." Her thick gold bangles clang with the motion when she beckons me closer. She puts a hand under my elbow and guides me to the stairs.

Back before she married Appa, she was the one who defended

me against Amma's tantrums. "She's an active child," she'd say. "I used to climb trees all the time too. Don't worry." She talked Amma down from punishing me for scraping up my knees, for ripping holes in my jeans, for holding hands with a boy after school. In third grade I asked for Barbie dolls for my birthday because I'd played with a friend's and I liked dressing them, with their poreless faces and plastic tan breasts. Instead, Laila Aunty got me a Lego set and some books, and told me that successful women need more than beauty. She was my favorite of all of our family friends. But that was before the divorce, before I took sides.

"You and your husband are getting along, no?" she says.

"Yes, yes, of course."

She stops with one foot on the stairs.

"We're fine," I say.

"Fighting is a part of married life, Lucky."

Amma and Appa fought all the time when I was young.

She sighs. "You can't let it break you."

⌒

Upstairs, Kris is drunk. He slurs his Tamil words and gives me a vacant look when I walk into the living room. He raises his glass. I sit next to him on the couch, the bourbon still tingling inside me.

The men are in a heated debate about the election, some of them arguing that Romney's tax plans would benefit them because they're in a higher tax bracket, even though we all know everyone here will vote for Obama.

"You need whiskey to join this conversation, Lucky," one of the men says.

They all laugh, because the idea of a woman drinking whiskey is just too absurd.

Kris chuckles to himself and drains the last sip from his glass. He shakes a piece of yellow-stained ice into his mouth. His arm slithers around my waist.

I slap his hand away. He tries again. I think about Nisha's cold fingers under my saree. I take Kris's hand off my waist and put it back on his knee. I twist his fingers just a little too hard. Appa gives me a look, but none of the other men notice our fight.

Kris stares at his whiskey glass like he's expecting it to refill itself. He doesn't talk to me the rest of the night, not until we're in the car and driving back to Amma's house. He insists that he be seen driving away from the party, like all the other drunk brown men who don't trust their wives with cars. Once we're a few blocks away, he pulls over into a gas station and we switch seats in the chilly night air.

"Are you going to ignore me all night?" I say. I wonder if he's still mad that I twisted his fingers.

He rubs his hands together and blows into them. Steam curls up from his mouth, fading into the darkness of the car.

"You know I hate it when you get all touchy," I say.

"I'm supposed to touch you. You're my wife."

I keep my eyes on the road, anger filling me up in the space the bourbon left behind. "I'm not your fucking wife. I'm not your puppet you can use to make a point."

Kris gets quiet, and when he speaks again I have to strain to hear him over the hum of the car. "We're all puppets. That's all we are."

"Stop it, Kris."

"I'm your puppet, too."

"Stop it."

"Because of me," he says, his voice rising a fraction, "you can seem like the perfect little brown wife."

I check the rearview mirror. No one behind us. I slam the brakes, hurtling Kris forward into his seatbelt. I drive on.

"Jesus, look at us," he says. A passing Dunkin' Donuts sign bathes him in its orange glow. "Let's get coffee."

I pull into the drive-thru. We get our coffees with milk and sugar and drink them in the car. I wait for a long expanse of silence, revving myself up to say it. Finally I say into the cold of the car, "I fucked Nisha. A couple of weeks ago."

Kris turns and looks at me. His eyebrows shoot up. He takes another sip of coffee and fights to keep a smile off his face.

"It's not funny," I say.

He slips a cigarette out of his pocket. He likes to pretend he smokes, but no matter how many he might tuck away, he isn't addicted. He wants to be. So he keeps on doing it, hoping that one day he'll get that urge that smokers talk about.

"Justin's been staying with me while you've been gone," he says. Justin is his on-again, off-again boyfriend of two years. "He's been talking about moving to California. He wants me to go with him."

"You can't." It's silly to say. I'm not his wife.

He spits out sweet, clove-flavored smoke as he speaks. "I won't. I told him no."

⁓

That night, Amma insists on sleeping in the guest bedroom so that Kris and I can have her bed. When Kris leaves the next morning, Amma says, "You two are fighting." She's cooking, talking to the giant nonstick wok that she loves to use.

"He had to go into the office," I say. That was his excuse. I think he just wanted to see Justin before California becomes a reality.

I'm cutting up onions. Amma doesn't trust me with the actual cooking. When I was in high school she didn't even trust me to use a knife without slipping and cutting off my finger, so instead I had to rinse all the vegetables and pull skin off the chicken.

Amma comes up and peers over my shoulder. "Cut them small."

"I *am* cutting them small."

She grabs the knife from me and butts me out of the way with her hip. "Small," she says. She cuts a few strips, each impossibly thin and transparent as glass.

"That'll take forever."

"It'll taste better."

I try to cut the onions as thin as she had, but my knife slides down the exposed edge of the onion without stripping it.

"We're not fighting," I say.

"Get the leeks out."

I grab the leeks from the fridge and wash them.

"Do you know how to cut leeks?"

"Why wouldn't I know?"

I don't actually. But I'm not going to tell her that. She'd go on for hours about how she doesn't know how Kris can put up with a wife who doesn't even know how to cut leeks.

"We're not fighting," I say.

"Cut the leeks small, too."

I cut the leeks smaller, thinner, sliding the knife down again and again, cutting off pieces as thin as string, watching the morning light glint off the metal edge. One slip, and the leeks could be red.

After the engagement party, Nisha doesn't talk to me. But just a week later she comes by the house while Amma's at work.

"I didn't think you'd answer your phone," she says when I open the door.

"I wouldn't have."

She pushes past me and into the house. She keeps her blue peacoat on and her hands in her pockets. "Let's go somewhere," she says.

I point to Grandmother, sitting outside on the deck.

"I can't leave her here," I say.

Nisha looks around the entryway. "Do you need me to pose for something?" She peers around the wall at my laptop and the reference photos scattered all over the couch. My half-colored commission of a pixie looks back at her. Only the pixie's skin is colored so far—a dark almond that clashes sharply with the still-white background. The young man who ordered the drawing didn't specify a skin color, but I know he meant for her to be pale. It's my policy to default brown skin when the commissioner doesn't specify.

"The line art's done," I say. Three more commissions have come in since I last saw Nisha, but all those are custom portraits—easy, painless, fast. The pixie is supposed to look like an oil painting, and the budget, I was promised, is unlimited. "Don't you have class?"

She scrunches up her nose. "This weekend then. Let's go out." She steps closer.

"I don't think—"

She puts a finger on the edge of my clavicle and traces it slowly. "Come on, Lucky. You're still my best friend."

⌒

Amma isn't keen on the idea.

"Where are you going to go?" she asks. She squints at the computer and enters credit card receipts into a spreadsheet.

"I don't know."

"You have to be careful. Not everywhere is safe."

"Amma—"

"Why don't you ask Nisha to come here for dinner?"

"She wants to go out."

Amma's lips press into a thin line. "When you're home you should spend time with your family."

I haven't left the house for weeks. I want to punch something. Twenty-seven years old and married. I own a house and car, and I have to ask my mother permission to leave her home.

Amma doesn't say anything. She flattens out a receipt between her fingers and enters the total into the computer. I wait a little longer for her to say something, and when she doesn't, I take that as permission.

Nisha drives me to Jamaica Plain, to a house where some of her friends from Wellesley—her first college—live. She's tense and quiet, her shoulders pulled back, her hands in the ten and two position, her eyes on the road. I keep quiet. She doesn't like the closeness of the other cars, the traffic, the road rage. Makes her nervous. I watch the river. One flick of the wheel.

We pull up to a faded gray triple-decker with a porch so large it overwhelms the front. Three mismatched old parlor chairs overlook the sharp incline of a one-way street. Other houses in the neighborhood still have flowers in their lawns and tough hedges that hide cracked foundations, but this house is unadorned except for the mailbox, which is painted with blue and yellow squares.

Nisha checks her makeup in the rear view mirror and coats her lips with a sparkly pink gloss. When she smiles at me, her lips catch the sun and glisten like water. The wind plucks leaves from the trees and scatters them over the dappled sky. I follow her up the steep wooden stairs to the deck. She knocks. No answer. She yells through the blue curtains that hang limp in the half-open windows. The door opens and a solidly-built white woman with a crew cut sweeps Nisha up into a hug.

"Jesse," the woman greets me. She extends a hand and I shake it. "Welcome to the Wellesley rugby house." She moves aside and points the way.

The house is even older from the inside. Exposed beams crisscross the ceiling around a rainbow American flag. Deep cracks spread over dark blue walls like varicose veins. An open hallway leads to two cherrywood doors and a yellow-tiled kitchen. There's a musty smell I can't place, like weeks-old sweat. Three women around my age cluster on low couches around a TV. In a corner underneath a bookcase that holds artwork, two people snooze on a single-person bed, covered in a rainbow tie-dyed quilt.

All the women are dressed in polos, black biking shorts, and gym shorts with the same blue and yellow checkerboard pattern as the mailbox outside. Some have cleats hung over their shoulders.

Someone stirs on the bed and says, "We have new people." A dark head with kinky black hair pokes out of the sheets and looks at me.

The women introduce themselves one by one and shake hands with me, their grips strong like mine. How the hell is Nisha friends with these women?

The curly-haired black woman wiggles out of the bed and introduces herself as Tasha.

"We're playing in the park today," she says. "Are you playing?"

"Not me," Nisha says.

Tasha turns to me. "How about you, handsome? Fancy some rugby?"

Handsome. No one's ever used that word to describe me before.

"I don't play rugby," I say.

Everyone gathers their things and tromps out to a park down the hill. The women spread out on the field in between the fenced-in playground equipment and the brick subway station, scouring the grass, picking up sticks and cigarette butts. They change into their cleats and mark the four corners of a rectangle with their shoes.

I sit on a cold wire bench with Nisha and Tasha, whose cleats still dangle on her shoulder and smell like a hundred feet.

The women jog around the rectangle they've marked. One pulls out a ball from a backpack—big and oblong like a swollen football. They form a circle with their backs facing the center and pass the ball to each other. Step to the side and pass. Step and pass. Step, pass.

"Why don't you play?" Tasha asks me. "Do you want to?" She has sharp eyes and a long, hooked nose like a songbird. She unzips the backpack at her feet, pulls out another rugby ball, and walks over to the corner of the field. She has a slight limp.

I follow. She looks at Nisha, but Nisha's intently watching the other women as they lift each other up by their shorts.

Tasha teaches me how to throw the ball by stepping to the side. We pass the ball back and forth. "You're pretty good," she says. She waves her arms at the women on the field. "Yo! Lucky here should play with you."

"I don't know the rules." I hope I'm not blushing. I never was a sports kid. I may have been a good dancer, but team sports made me uncoordinated and awkward.

"The best way to learn rugby is by playing. Our feet look about the same size." She holds out her cleats.

Jesse takes me aside and narrates the rules to me while the others play. "This is a scrimmage," she says. "Or scrum."

Two women face each other and hook arms over shoulders. Someone calls "go" and they push against each other, the ball on the ground beneath them.

"A scrum restarts play. Usually you'll have all the forwards stacked against each other. In rugby sevens, you have three against three. In rugby league laws, you get six on six. Rugby union, eight on eight."

One of the women pushes the other backward. The ball emerges.

"Want to try?" Jesse doesn't wait for me to answer. She holds up an arm and the others stop playing. We walk out onto the field.

Jesse faces me, tips forward, hooks her arm around me, and presses the top of her head on my shoulder. I imitate her, get a lung-full of sweat smell. We're locked. I feel steady in this position, solid. Someone puts the ball underneath us.

"Now push with your legs," she says.

Before I'm ready, she pushes forward. My legs skid back. I push.

"Keep pushing."

I'm out of shape, and no match for her. She's twice my size, and probably four times my muscle density. She pushes me backward until someone picks up the ball from behind her.

"Not bad," Jesse says. "With some practice you could play for real."

"I couldn't push you back."

"Yeah, but I'm a beast. Against someone smaller you'll be fine."

We play three on three. Tasha shouts the rules to me while I run from one side of the field to the other and try to keep track of who's on my team. I don't fumble the ball. Sometimes it's cradled against my side. I run down the field and it's like I haven't breathed properly for ages. My legs run despite the ache in my muscles. Whenever someone gets close to me I can smell the sweat caked into her uniform, old and stale. I can feel the blood in my skin, the tendons pushing and pulling at my limbs. The others tackle each other, crashing to the ground all limbs and skin. I want to be part of the mess, wonderful chaos and movement, a purpose I haven't felt in my muscles for much too long. I haven't danced in ages and this is like scratching an itch deep under the skin. I remember what it's like to move—like something ballooning inside of me, like I'm going to expand and expand and become the air.

We play until we can't see each other's faces in the darkening night. Goosebumps coat my legs and the back of my neck. I shiver even in my jeans and long-sleeved shirt. On the walk home, Tasha pats me on the back and says, "You should play more with us."

Nisha saunters past Jesse, laughing and tossing her hair.

"I see," Tasha says, watching me. "You and Nisha."

I nod and hope it looks nonchalant. I watch Nisha out of the corner of my eye.

Tasha drapes an arm over my shoulder. "You're welcome at the rugby house anytime you feel like coming."

We buy beer from a liquor store with large windows and wooden racks of wine bottles. "It's not rugby without a social," Jesse says. When I try to give her money she waves it away. "You played a damn good game."

At the house we pass around a laptop and pick music—mostly obscure girl-with-guitar melodies that collapse over syncopated strumming. I want something with stronger, more regular bass, something I can keep inside my bones. Every once in a while someone picks hip-hop or punk and I can feel it like a heartbeat inside of me.

Nisha sits back against the wall and drinks a wine cooler. I still can't believe that she knows these women. I scoot closer. She pulls me by the collar and kisses me. The women hoot and raise their drinks. Nisha pushes me away and laughs, like it's all a joke.

Tasha clinks her beer bottle and the music turns off. Jesse stands up and sings, one hand on her heart and the other raised in the air toward the ceiling and the rainbow American flag. "Oh, my lover's a lawyer, a lawyer, a lawyer, a mighty fine lawyer is she-ee!" The women laugh and join in. Their voices rise in a drunken heap. "All day long she fucks you, she fucks you, she fucks you"—Jesse points at each of us in turn—"and when she gets home she fucks me."

They all stand up and make a line behind Jesse. Tasha motions for me to join them but Nisha's holding my hand and I don't ever want to move. The women march to the beat and sing. "You've got to live a little bit, love a little bit, follow the band. Follow the band with your tits in your hand—wah wah!"

And Nisha watches all this like she's seen it before. Nisha, who at Sri Lankan parties says all the right things and moves like a Bollywood princess, who has perfected the coy downward glance of a proper brown woman. She lets me kiss her.

Once or twice during the night, the rugby girls get into brawls, holding each other in headlocks or wrestling on the floor. Tasha keeps inviting me to join in, and just when I'm starting to relax enough to try, Nisha stands up to leave.

"My parents texted," she says. "They're wondering where I am."

Forty minutes later, she pulls up to the end of Emerson Drive where the road turns into a makeshift driveway. Was this a date? She waits for me to get out.

I feel like I should say something. "Thanks for taking me. I had fun. Are you sure you can't come in?" I touch her wrist on the steering wheel. She tenses and I draw away. "Sorry," I say.

"I can't." She looks at the house and its lit upstairs windows. I start to get out.

"Wait." She gives me a peck on the mouth.

I watch her drive off. The moon waxes full and eerie. If I were someone else, in some other story, I'd take a midnight walk with my wife.

Amma's waiting up for me. I hope she won't notice the beer on my breath, or the lip gloss from Nisha's kiss. I go straight to bed, ignoring Amma at the kitchen table reading her favorite swami's scripture.

Appa wants me over for dinner. I change three times before Amma finally gives my outfit a nod. She pulls my hair into a tiny, frizzy ponytail and makes me wear jewelry.

"A woman should never go bare," she says. "A woman should always wear gold."

Grandmother watches Tamil soap operas from her folding chair in the living room. Every once in a while she glances at the deck.

I drink tea in the kitchen and try to prepare myself for the lemon disinfectant and vinyl sofa covers of Laila Aunty's house.

"Be good," Amma says.

Grandmother opens the sliding glass doors. A cold breeze sucks itself into the vacuum of the house.

"Close the door," Amma says.

Grandmother hobbles to the kitchen and picks up her tea from the counter. Amma goes to close the door.

"We need to prepare for the baby," Grandmother says. She coughs and smiles.

Amma freezes.

"The baby is coming soon."

"What baby?" Amma asks.

"Vidya's baby."

Amma's flesh tenses. Her face goes rigid like it does whenever someone mentions Vidya. She shuts the sliding glass doors with a snap.

Grandmother points at me. "Vidya is having a baby."

Amma walks back to the kitchen and picks up her chipped mug of tea. "That's Lucky." Her voice rises on my name. "What's this about a baby?"

I take a big gulp of too-hot tea.

"You're having a baby?"

"Yes, yes," Grandmother says.

"No," I say.

"You should be thinking about it," Amma says.

"About what?"

"Having a baby."

If this is the conversation we're going to have, I'd rather be at Laila Aunty's lemon-disinfectant house. I push my way to the foyer and throw on my jacket.

"I'm serious, Lucky."

I kneel and tie my shoes.

"You need to throw those away." Amma points to the faded blue high tops on my feet.

I make a double knot in my shoelaces.

"Kris is a good-looking man," she says. "You need to give him a baby soon."

I get up and head for the door without looking at her. I make sure to slam it just a little harder than I need to.

~

Laila Aunty and Appa live in a renovated yellow colonial that dwarfs Amma's house, though it's considered small for their neighborhood. The house is set back from the road, obscured by old trees that make you feel like you're completely alone inside.

Laila Aunty opens the door half-dressed in a silk saree and plants a sticky kiss on my cheek.

"Come, come." She walks toward the living room where Appa is reading the *Boston Globe* from his favorite chair. "We're going to temple, dear," she says. "I'm just getting ready."

"I didn't bring any clothes for temple."

"I got you something from that new store in New Jersey. You can wear that." She disappears down the hallway.

I sit on the hard, powder-green sofa. The cleanliness of the house is unnerving. Thick brown draperies block out the light, fleurs-de-lis dot the thick white carpet, wooden sculptures of dancing women crowd every flat surface—I feel like there's not enough oxygen in the room. Amma is minimalist by comparison. Dealing only in necessities is a habit she cultivated from her poor childhood.

My mother's family came here on a lottery visa, back when the U.S. had compassion for Sri Lankan refugees. Her name came out of a hat, so she survived the war. Her two older brothers were detained at the airport in Sri Lanka, suspected of being terrorists, so it was a little family of three that landed at JFK airport, via Dubai, via Hong Kong.

My father came here on a graduate student visa. Immigration policies re-create heightened natural selection. The smartest and those with the most resources make it out, along with a handful of those who just get lucky. Amma's luck ran out, but Appa's resources stayed intact.

Laila Aunty comes back with a bag that smells of sandalwood, and dumps the contents next to me on the couch: a baby-pink mirrored tunic with pale-yellow drawstring pants, a necklace, and matching pink and yellow bangles. Of course she'd buy me such dainty colors. Everyone does.

I dress in their guest bedroom. The new churidar scratches against my ribcage. Laila Aunty irons her saree into knifelike pleats, then combs and pulls my hair into something resembling a bun, held together with a thousand bobby pins because it isn't long enough.

The Sri Lakshmi temple is a half hour away. When I was little I always called it my temple because the main deity is my namesake. I am named after a Hindu goddess sometimes pictured massaging her husband's shins as he sleeps. Lakshmi, the goddess of wealth and beauty, but I wasn't born into either one. Every time Lakshmi's husband Vishnu takes a human form, she does too. But sometimes Vishnu incarnates as a woman, usually in order to seduce men. And then what does Lakshmi do? Sit up in heaven and try not to watch? Or maybe she does, maybe she finds herself drawn to his new soft curves. Maybe she wants to unwrap him and fit her hand into the fold of his waist.

Appa drives while Laila Aunty fusses with her saree. Somewhere near the exit for Ashland, she whips around in her seat.

"You don't have a pottu," she says. "We can't go to temple with you looking like that." She digs in her purse and pulls out red lipstick. She spins a dot in between my eyebrows and turns back around.

Set sharply off the road, the stark white temple overlooks suburban sprawl from atop a hill. It grows from the tops of trees as we turn onto a side street. White plaster sculptures pose inside the walls. In Sri Lanka and India, temples are painted bright and clashing colors, but this one is frozen in perpetual construction, its three white spires just recently topped with gold cones that jut into the sky.

Appa circles the parking lot twice before he pulls his BMW into an empty spot at the bottom of the hill. It's Saturday, meaning everyone is here. Laila Aunty thrives on the crowded energy. I'd rather avoid it. She steps out of the car with her back straight and her stomach sucked in. She pulls up the pleats of her saree so that the drape of cotton covers her chest.

We walk slowly up the hill to the temple. Laila Aunty struggles behind us because of her net-ball-player knee problems from college. Or because she is now as soft and wifelike as Amma wants me to be. We wait for her under the carport where people park new cars to be blessed. The asphalt underneath is littered with smashed limes that were placed under car tires to be run over for luck. Appa holds the door open and I can tell his back has give to it now, not as straight as I remember it.

I know my way around this temple by heart, know that there are two cement steps up to the landing before the doors where everyone takes off their shoes, the white marble antechamber where people hang coats in messy rows, the floor sink with the motion detector faucet where the truly religious wash their hands and feet before stepping inside the main temple. The interior unfolds into an airy main chamber with cool marble floors. Small shrines line the walls, each under their own plaster canopy. The idols wear miniature silk clothes and regular-sized jewelry that hangs down to their knees. Every once in a while a worshipper rings the bell hanging by the main shrine. The sound echoes on the marble and makes babies cry. Fathers pick up their children so they can ring the bell. No one pays me any mind.

The main shrine stands tall and center, completely enclosed. Lakshmi's chamber is probably around the size of Laila Aunty's walk-in closet, separated from the worshippers by two sets of thick wooden doors. Only priests are allowed inside.

I watch the women as they circle around the shrines. Women aren't allowed to be priests, but they seem more saintly than the men inside the white walls of the temple, wrapped up like many beautiful presents—the exposed expanses of their backs, the flesh that ripples over their shoulders, the way their spines curve and dip into their lower backs. In ancient India, before the British outlawed the practice, temples employed and housed dancers. Families pledged their daughters to the temple to be given an education in the arts after a marriage ceremony where a god statue stood in for the groom. These devdasis enjoyed the privileges of a married woman in society but answered to no man. They weren't expected to remain chaste or give up their careers to become housewives.

Children chase each other around, silent at their parents' scolding looks, like little muted movies. Infants sleep in carriers near the support columns at the corners of the temple. The air fills with spicy sweet incense that my white friends in high school told me smelled like weed—they had huddled around the doorway of my parents' prayer room, sniffing the air with round eyes and smiles at the corners of their mouths. Many of them asked me to take them to temple. I never did.

I follow Appa around the shrines. We make a faster route than Laila Aunty, who lumbers from shrine to shrine with her palms clasped together, her lips moving furiously. She's a real believer. We circle around each shrine three times, stop to touch the carvings at each cardinal direction, count nine careful circles around the shrine of the planet gods. I stop in front of each shrine to pray with my palms together, but not for so long I get bored. The dark idols watch me with vacant eyes. I don't know what to pray for.

The jingle of bells signals the beginning of pooja. Everyone gets into two lines at the open doors of the main shrine. The priest is naked and hairy down to his waist. A thin white thread loops around one shoulder and travels diagonally down his chest. He wears a dhoti wrapped around his legs to make shorts. Laila Aunty holds out fruit and flowers on a tin platter. The priest asks her for names and horoscope signs so that he can pray for us. He takes the flowers and fruits inside the main chamber of the shrine. His Sanskrit chants fill the temple. He throws flowers one by one onto the dark stone idol of Lakshmi.

I line up behind Appa. Laila Aunty joins the other line. The priest brings out a thick silver tray with little copper containers and a lit oil lamp. He walks down one line, dipping into each container for each person. I hold out my palms, my right on top of my left. The priest puts a pinch of veebuthi in the center of my palm. I dip my finger in and rub a line across my forehead. The rest settles gritty into the crevices of my palms. The priest spoons clear liquid into my palm. I drink it, the sweet water mixed with the remnants of veebuthi, and wipe the rest onto my head. I hold my hands over the flame of the oil lamp and press the warmth into my brow. The priest drops two almonds and three raisins into my palm. He moves on to the next person in line, down one side of the aisle and up the other.

Appa and I escape down the staircase to the basement where the food is sold while Laila Aunty finishes. He buys two boxes of lemon rice and one box of yogurt rice with lime pickle. My favorite. We find seats on cold metal folding chairs set up haphazardly in the open room.

"Laila Aunty will be mad," I say. "We prayed too fast." I take a bite of my yogurt rice and the ratio of pickle to rice is perfect. The yogurt spreads thick in my mouth, the lime pickle biting and sour.

Appa's plastic fork hangs limp. "Nisha wants to see you. She's having trouble with the marriage idea."

I can feel the sweat in my armpits, soaking into the cotton sleeves of my churidar top. I dig at the lime wedge in my rice.

"You girls," he says. "You American girls get so scared for no reason."

Maybe I should've prayed for Nisha. I imagine her in a heavy red wedding saree, her hair done up with flowers and jewels cascading down her chest. Nisha, with a nose ring and bangles stacked to her elbows. Nisha, walking into her husband's bedroom on her wedding night.

When Laila Aunty finally comes down to join us, she has angry pink patches on her cheeks. The room crowds fast, sweltering with heat. We go outside for air.

"What did you pray for, Lucky?" she asks. "You must always

pray for something. I prayed for my daughters to have good heads. And for you to start acting more like a woman."

In ancient India, devdasis were a revered and respected part of temple tradition. But the British saw the practice of women trained in the arts, free to take on lovers, as prostitution. For many years after that, dancing was considered shameful in Indian culture. It's only lately that Bharatanatyam has seen a revival. If Nisha and I were devdasis back then, back before the British, we might have been free. I could pray, but here's the truth: even if the gods are real, I don't think they can liberate us.

HEART OF STONE

One day Amma comes home from work early and sees Grandmother sitting on the porch.

"It's freezing out there," Amma says. "How can you be so irresponsible?"

"She likes it out there."

"She's restless. You need to take her for an outing."

"Where?"

Amma dumps the contents of her lunch bag into the sink. "Don't ask me. Take some responsibility."

I ask Grandmother. She wants to go to an art museum. When I was younger and Grandmother still lived with Amma's sister-in-law in Sri Lanka, we would go to the museum whenever she visited. Vidya, then a teenager, came with us. Vidya and I would bring our sketchbooks in identical messenger bags and try to sketch out the paintings we liked. Once they had a visiting exhibit featuring photographs of Bharatanatyam dancers. I walked around the room for hours, sitting on the benches and trying to draw the dancers' curves. My child hands cramped up and my fingers refused to move, until Vidya took my hand and showed me how to sketch with my arm as a brush. "Art isn't small," she said. "Don't try to fit it into your fist."

Nisha wants to go with us. I dress Grandmother in a saree because she refuses to leave the house in anything else. I push her feet into sandals and buckle the straps. She leans heavily on me as she walks out to the car.

"We could use the wheelchair," I say. I've loaded it into the trunk.

She shakes her head. Her spine stands a little taller. I help her into the backseat and she buckles her seat belt. I put her walking stick on her lap.

We pick up Nisha on the way. I play Grandmother's favorite CD of calm, melodious Tamil music from the sixties, and she drifts off to sleep. Nisha holds my hand as I drive. Her thumb makes little circles on the back of my palm.

Grandmother hobbles from the parking garage to the museum. She won't even lean on me for support. She uses her walking stick and stands with her head high, looking more like a schoolteacher than ever, her white hair in a bun at the nape of her neck. Her eyes are clear, eager.

Nisha and I trail behind her. Nisha walks closer to me than normal, her arms brushing mine.

In front of the museum, a homeless woman sits against a tree. Grandmother stops. She pulls out the small coin purse she wears tucked into the waistband of her saree, counts out three dollar bills and a nickel, and drops them into the woman's outstretched Au Bon Pain cup.

As we walk away, Grandmother says to me, "Always help out the beggars who sit outside temples."

"This is a museum, Ammamma."

She smiles and pats my cheek. "Come, Vidya. Let's go practice your art."

We let her lead. Instead of heading toward the MFA, she turns and walks toward the Isabella Stewart Gardner Museum. She's always liked it better, with its rooms arranged like a house, ready for afternoon tea. Halfway there, she stops to rest on a park bench and watches geese eat grass. Green blades stick to their beaks as they waddle from patch to patch.

"How can she know the way to the museum but still call you Vidya?" Nisha asks.

"She always came here with Vidya."

"And you."

Nisha buys tickets while I check our coats and bags. Grandmother looks up through the glass walls of the entrance. I wonder if she remembers the way through the museum. We used to spend hours wandering the rooms. When I was younger, I imagined that ghosts still roamed the halls, going about their business as usual, arranging their hair in front of the smoky mirrors, having tea on the silk sofas, entertaining guests with a piano concert in the Tapestry Room.

Grandmother uses her walking stick as we go through the glass corridor to the historic building. I take it in, the arched brick doorways, the courtyard with gothic windows reaching up to the glass roof, the sound of falling water and people's hushed conversations. My muscles relax of their own accord. I hadn't even realized they were tense.

Nisha helps Grandmother sit down on a stone bench.

"Go on," Grandmother says. "Go see the dancer."

She remembers. I walk down into the Spanish Cloister, with its ceramic-tiled walls and scalloped stone archway. Life-sized and framed, it's as if the whole room was built just to house this painting. *El Jaleo*. The ruckus. A woman dances flamenco while black-suited men play guitars in the background. One man arches his head back. The dancer tilts at an impossible angle, her hand pointing toward the courtyard, volumes of fabric cascading off her hip. When I was younger I tried to sketch it, but my figure always seemed too stiff, too posed.

I wish I'd brought a sketchpad to try now. Maybe I'm ready. I watch the painting for a while longer. My back unknots.

When I join Grandmother, she's dozing against Nisha's shoulder. I shake her gently.

"Ammamma? Are you ready to go?"

She snaps awake and looks confused. "Did we see the paintings?"

"Not yet."

She blinks clarity into her eyes and stands up. We walk through the Yellow Room, one of her favorite places, where a mirror lets us watch ourselves watch the paintings. *Nocturne, Blue and Silver: Battersea Reach*. The Blue Room, with its striped wallpaper and dainty sofas. A pale woman against the dawn, her red hair blowing in the wind. *The Shower of Gold*.

I wonder if Grandmother can remember the paintings' names she used to help me memorize. Her face slides in and out of attention as we walk. At the bottom of the stairs, she turns to me.

"Help me climb," she says.

"There's an elevator."

"I don't want anyone's pity."

So I help her climb the stairs. We walk through the Dutch Room, where twenty years ago a pair of thieves sliced five paintings out with box cutters. The gilded frames still hang against the filigree wallpaper, empty. Grandmother has always loved this room. Every time we walked through she would say the same thing. I wonder if she'll say it now.

Hobbling out of the room on her walking stick, she says, "It's always about the ones who aren't here. Remember that."

The sentiment seems to be one that every Sri Lankan understands implicitly, we who start every cultural function with a moment of silence for those lost in our country's decades-long ethnic civil war. Never forget the empty chairs. Never forget who should've been here.

"Vidya," Grandmother says. "Let's go to the church."

The church is the Long Gallery on the third floor with a stained glass window on one side and small pews where people can kneel to pray. I help Grandmother kneel. She folds her palms one over the other and prays. Nisha does the same.

I stand behind them. I don't even know how to pray at the temple. How do I pray in a museum?

Nisha crosses herself and stands up. She walks backward and takes my arm.

"Do you want to know what I prayed about?" she asks. With a glance toward Grandmother, she kisses me on the cheek.

"That you won't get married?"

I say it as a joke but she says, "I prayed for a way out of this."
She sighs and rests her head on my shoulder.

There's always a way out. You could be a ghost. I could be
an empty chair.

"Don't you want to sketch anything?" she asks.

"I didn't bring a sketchbook."

"Wait here." She jogs out of the room. By the time I help
Grandmother stand again, Nisha is back. She pushes a small
notebook and pencil into my hands. "I'll help Grandmother
walk around. Go sketch."

I can't kiss her in front of Grandmother but I smile and hope
it's enough. I take the notebook back to the Spanish Cloister
and sit down on a bench. The room is shadowed. Slivers of
light float in from the garden and the courtyard, but the stone
pillars and floor absorb most of it. The grays and blacks of the
painting shift and slide around in my vision. What must it be
like for the dancer, in front of all those men? Did she use her
body as a way to keep them back?

I make a few false starts. The pencil is much too small. I
adjust, and the fourth sketch captures her movement. She isn't
falling. She's simply dancing, simply moving. I sketch. There's
no wedding. No Nisha. No museum. Just the dance. A way to
keep them back. A movement like falling but you never crash.

The windows of Machine pulse with light that spills onto drunk passersby. A motley group of club-goers waits outside in line—androgynous youngsters with pierced noses, aging twinks with bright hair, hard and soft femmes in flirty dresses. Others rest against the brick of the neighboring mattress store to smoke.

I sit in my parked car and wait for Nisha. Bruins fans pass me in droves. She was supposed to be here fifteen minutes ago.

When she finally arrives, her knock on the car window makes me jump.

I get out of the car. "What took you?"

Her makeup is stronger than usual, her eyes lined and her lips red. Her hipbones jut out over her tight jeans.

I smooth down my UMass Minutemen shirt and try to

run my hands through my hair. She tucks some strands behind my ears.

"You look nice," I say.

She hooks her spangled purse under her arm. Her wrists clang with bangles. The line at the entrance thins out by the time we join in. A cute butch in front of us smiles at Nisha. I put an arm around her waist. Her T-shirt is cut in such a way that I can touch the skin of her lower back.

The bouncer at the door seems to know Nisha. She nods to us as she stamps our wrists. The bass of the dance beat resets my heart. We walk downstairs to a bar. Darkness crawls inside our eyes. People play pool and arcade games, and inside a glass-paneled room, a massive crowd dances to techno. Nisha walks to the bar and leans against it so that her hips tilt at just the right angle. The light arcs over her butt.

"Cosmo, strong," she says to the bartender.

"Beer," I say. "Whatever you have."

The bartender puts down two glasses. Nisha takes hers and sips, so I pay for the drinks. Men in tight Hollister shirts laugh and bend toward each other at the pool tables. Women in shorts stand around in large groups at the tables. One woman in baggy cargoes and a striped polo smiles at me from a corner of the bar.

Nisha stays quiet and watches the crowd. The music is so loud I wouldn't be able to hear her anyway. She stands next to a poster advertising for dancers at a club called the Mason Jar. My beer tastes like perfume. I should've been more careful about what I ordered. I take in the chill of the air conditioning that falls down from black vents in the ceiling. I've heard of this place but I've never been. How many times has Nisha come here? How many women has she brought?

"Do you always come here?" I ask.

The woman across the bar is still watching me, her flat-billed hat tilted slightly on her head.

"Not always."

The woman across the bar lifts her beer in a toast and takes a drink. I drink from my glass.

"Are you listening?"

"What?"

Nisha pouts. She pulls my hand. "I used to come in college. Let's go dance."

The dance floor is so crowded we can't move. Nisha pushes through and pulls me behind her. Someone's sweaty back grazes my arm. Someone else's elbow bumps me in the small of my back. But the beat is sinking into me. Nisha rubs her palms on mine and pulls me closer. I close my eyes against the pulsing lights. Dark. Jasmine. Nisha. I press my fingers into her waist. Skin. She breathes against my neck.

"I'm so glad you came," she says. "I miss this."

"You don't have to get married."

She draws back and looks at my face. The light glints off her blue contacts.

"Of course I have to," she says. "I meant I miss not having to pretend."

I see the woman from before, the one with the flat-billed hat, over Nisha's shoulder. She smiles, and jerks her head toward the exit.

"If you get married," I say, "you'll have to pretend forever."

Nisha's palms twitch on my spine. "Pretending is better than the alternative."

I push her off of me. "I'm going to the bathroom." I walk in that general direction until I'm sure Nisha can't see me, then climb up the steps toward the exit.

Bruins fans stumble around outside the club. People smoke beside the buildings. Butts litter the concrete.

The woman is waiting for me, twirling a cigarette in her fingers. She moves closer and offers me one. I take it, just in case Nisha happens to wander this way and wonder what I'm doing. The woman lights it and steps close enough that I can smell her cologne.

"That your girlfriend?" She tilts her head toward the club entrance.

"Not really." I hope my voice doesn't shake.

She raises an eyebrow. We smoke in silence, her shoulder almost close enough to mine that I can feel the air in between us. I should give this woman my number. Kris would say so. In a way she reminds me of the rugby girls, swagger and boyish charm. I don't owe Nisha anything.

"I have to go." I put out the cigarette with my foot.

The woman kisses my cheek. "Come see me if you change your mind."

I go back into the darkness of the club and down into the bathrooms. Four people in line. Good excuse for taking so much time. I fiddle with the edge of the poster calling for dancers at the Mason Jar. Female dancers experienced in belly dance, Middle Eastern or Indian dances, to work one night a week. I should've given my number to that woman. Nisha's engagement ceremony is around the corner. Female dancers, Indian dance, one night a week. Nisha's engagement, then the wedding. She'll be a wife before I know it. Before I can stop her. I don't even know if she wants me to stop her.

Amma is waiting up for me when I get home, her face bathed in the glow of her computer screen. She doesn't say anything. She makes me warm milk with sugar.

"I don't know what I did to deserve this," she says. She trudges up the stairs, leaving me to my milk.

Would it help if I told you Amma lost a baby? Her name was Tabu, and she was supposed to be born between my sister Vidya and me. But Tabu never cried. A year later Amma and Appa had me, so that I could walk in the shadows that Tabu's wrinkled little body never cast. Maybe Tabu would've made all the right decisions. Maybe Tabu would've made Amma happy.

In college my sister Shyama dated a man named Dave—a reserve Air Force staff sergeant who took night classes with her at Columbia—the type of man, she told me, who didn't believe in god or extraneous appliances. His Bronx apartment was sparse and clean. She liked it for its blankness. The walls were beige, the carpet was tan, and even with the paintings from the farmer's market that she eventually hung up, the place still looked bare with a minimum of furniture. A couch, a glass coffee table, and a bookcase that held a single row of mystery novels. Dave didn't have plants or animals, not even photos in frames. But he had a guitar that he practiced every night from six thirty to seven, and from nine to nine thirty. He ate dinner at seven fifteen, and went to bed at ten forty-five.

Shyama told me she didn't know if she loved him, only that he made her feel like she was doing something wrong. When in public, she wouldn't hold his hand. Amma, Appa and I lived only five hours away, and she had this fear that we would come to surprise her one day. So they stayed in Dave's apartment.

She knew it was coming. At every holiday when she visited home, she asked me if I'd heard Amma and Appa talking about her marriage. I always said no, but I never listened at their closed door. They sprung it on her when she came home for the summer after her junior year. I had no warning.

"Your uncle's wife," Amma said. "Her parents' neighbors have a nephew in Canada. He's thirty-two, an engineer."

Shyama's face went still. She looked at me. I stared at the dining table and tried to shrink into my seat.

"An engineer. He owns a house and everything."

Shyama picked up her suitcase and tried to walk up the stairs.

"A house, Shyama. That means he's responsible. A very good boy."

Shyama paused on the steps and turned around, still holding her suitcase. "You're serious?"

Amma's smile quivered. "You're getting old. You need a husband."

A year after Shyama got married, Amma and Appa split up, and Appa married Laila Aunty before the ink on the divorce papers dried. Maybe they knew it was coming. Maybe they hurried Shyama's arrangement so that her marriage could happen before theirs broke. No parents would send a son-in-law to a broken home.

"You can't walk through life alone," Appa said.

Shyama bit her lip. Was she thinking of Dave in his uniform? The summer would be too warm for all that heavy camouflage but that's how I always pictured him.

"You need someone to come home to," Amma said.

Appa coughed and put his hands in his pockets. "It's a good feeling. To know you have someone waiting for you at home."

Shyama had told me that girls in Dave's unit flirted with him all the time. She sometimes found their texts on his phone. He was too polite to say no. Amma and Appa would say that he wasn't a stable investment.

"He's in Toronto," Appa said. "His parents asked us to come see them."

Amma smiled large against Shyama's vacant look. "We're leaving this Friday."

Shyama couldn't sleep that night, just tossed and turned in the bed we shared as I hovered on the edge of sleep. Her phone conversations with Dave were short and clipped. She lay in bed with the blanket over her head and whispered into her phone. She didn't tell him about Canada. No mention of the arrangement. He was getting ready to ship out for annual training.

"You can do whatever you need to do," she told him.

"I miss you." His voice was muffled by the phone and blankets.

"You'll get over that."

"I love you."

"You may get over that, too."

When she wasn't talking to Dave, I tried to console her. "Maybe you can tell Amma and Appa about Dave," I said.

Shyama looked at me like I was crazy.

"It would stop them arranging things."

She frowned and looked away. "They'd kill me. This thing with Dave won't last forever."

"So you're just going to get married to someone else?"

"I can always say no to this guy."

"You have to fight for your relationship."

"You don't get it. There's no saying no. I say no to this one, it'll be another one, and then another, and then another."

"So you're going through with the arrangement."

Shyama's face still had that blank, unfocused look. "I'm not done fighting just yet."

Back then I believed in love, in forever. I would've done anything to fight for Nisha. But back then, Nisha didn't want to be fought for.

Appa emailed pictures of the engineer to Shyama. I watched over her shoulder. His name was Rajesh, and he posed in his house against stark white walls and landscape paintings in wooden frames. There he was standing next to his enormous oak dining table, his fifty-inch TV, his sports Audi. He wore suits and tight smiles in every picture. He had nervous eyes.

Appa insisted on driving the entire nine hours to Canada by himself because he didn't trust the women to drive well and no one insisted. Amma sat in the front seat and looked out the window while I sat squished between Shyama and Laila Aunty in the back. As Amma's widowed best friend, Laila Aunty was automatically invited to join us. In retrospect, it's hard to believe no one predicted Laila Aunty and Appa.

Except for the old Tamil songs that Appa played on repeat, the car stayed silent. When we stopped at rest areas, Amma pinched Shyama's cheeks and said, "Don't worry so much. He's a good boy."

Dave sent Shyama texts while he was on break from his

training sessions in Nebraska. She tilted her phone away from Laila Aunty, but I could still read most of them. He told her she was beautiful, that he missed her and that he loved her. He didn't seem like the kind of man to get over loving her.

We checked into our hotel rooms late that night. I shared a room with Shyama, so we opened the doors to the balcony and let the city in. A breeze wove through the metal bars of the railing. The balconies on the apartment building across the street burst with kids' bicycles and drying laundry, potted plants and worn wicker deck chairs, signs of immigrant families making a life. Toronto had comfort to it, like I could sink my toes in, with its strip malls of Tamil stores and ethnic fusion cuisine. I didn't know of any other place in the world where you could get Irish-Caribbean sushi with a side of refried beans and mango chutney.

"I wish you could come here," Shyama told Dave over the phone. She stood on the balcony with her back to me, scratching her calf with her big toe.

I tried to imagine Dave walking around the streets below, with his pasty skin and blonde hair, his Skechers shoes and tan cargo shorts like in the picture Shyama once showed me. White Canadians rarely ventured into immigrant areas. When we were younger, we played Spot the White People, and the one who saw the most won. Dave didn't belong here. Of that Shyama was right.

⁓

In Hinduism, the concept of dharma outlines the way you behave—the law of the universe, the amalgam of duties you hold as a sentient being made of stardust and god. The straight and narrow path. The right path. Dharma is the reason that people like Kris get married to people like me, the reason that Shyama gave up writing for graduate school, the reason that after the divorce, Amma is shunned at Sri Lankan gatherings while Appa is received with open arms.

The next morning Amma knocked on our door before we woke up, already fully dressed.

"Hurry up," she said, clucking her tongue. "We need to go shopping."

"For what?"

"Sarees."

Shyama pulled her blanket over her head.

"For you," Amma said, looking at her.

"I don't need sarees."

"Rajesh's parents are not going to meet you in those homeless-person jeans you wear. Don't be so lazy."

Before the store we stopped for breakfast at a Tamil shop. Shyama refused her dosai and sambar, even refused her coffee. Later, she wobbled in place and rubbed her eyes in the textile store entrance. The saree shop smelled like the back of Amma's armoire where she kept all her Indian clothing, a sweet musty smell that tickled the space between my ears. Glass shelves covered the walls of the store, holding what looked like thousands of sarees. Here and there stood jewelry holders with heavy necklaces and earrings.

Amma and Laila Aunty apparently knew the woman behind the counter. They talked pharmacy schools and husbands. Appa wandered off to look into the glass counters. I followed him and tried to be invisible. Shyama wasn't so lucky.

The woman slid behind the counter and pulled out sarees that she draped on Shyama's chest. The three women scrutinized each one.

"Too long. Makes her skin look dark."

"Blue is unlucky for a marriage."

"Too many sequins."

"Too plain."

"Which one do you like, Shyama?"

Shyama pointed to a green saree with brushstroke designs.

"That is not for young girls."

"Let her wear what she wants," Laila Aunty said.

"She will look old."

Did Laila Aunty know then that she was going to break our family apart? I wish I could remember if her gaze lingered too long on Appa, or if they shared secret smiles but I didn't know to look for it then.

Amma and Laila Aunty picked three sarees and two churidars. The sales woman cut out the blouse material from each one and took Shyama's measurements.

Next we headed to a jewelry shop that had floor-to-ceiling white bars under the glass, where we had to be buzzed inside. I looked at their display of nose rings while Amma and Laila Aunty weighed necklaces and earrings in their hands. Shyama checked her phone often.

"Do they always buy you so many things?" Dave asked that night when she told him about the sarees and jewelry. I pretended to be asleep while she talked to him. She was careful not to mention why we had come to Toronto.

"Daughters are supposed to have jewelry," she said. "It shows the family's wealth."

If it were me, I would've told him, if only to see if he stepped up to the challenge.

⁓

At night we ate takeout from the Sri Lankan store just blocks away from the hotel. String hoppers, sambol, mutton rolls, every kind of food we could hope for, wrapped in newspaper and offered for a couple dollars. Amma and Appa took Shyama so that she could practice her Tamil by ordering, even though she would barely touch the food—too much oil, too much coconut milk. She wanted to shrink down to fit her clothes from high school.

I stayed behind and drew on the balcony. The neighborhood of Scarborough sprawled out under me, its wide gridded roads, neon storefronts in Tamil and Mandarin, well-lit buses crawling along like glass beetles. I sketched loose and quick without thinking about composition or accuracy.

Laila Aunty found me, her hair still dripping from her shower. She stepped onto the balcony in her flip-flops.

"Why didn't you go with them, dear?" She peered over my shoulder at my drawing. "You've drawn the sky too cloudy, no?"

I looked up. The Toronto sky was clear except for a starved moon and pinprick stars. The sky I drew—clouds streaked across the graphite in a hurry to be elsewhere.

Laila Aunty leaned her elbows on the balcony railing. "What are you going to wear to their house tomorrow?"

"I'm sure Amma has something picked out." I shaded in the underside of the clouds.

"It's not so bad, you know." She watched the people on the sidewalk—Sri Lankans with skin indistinguishable from ours.

"I know."

"Your sister will be happy. She's a good girl. She'll adjust."

Laila Aunty had been widowed for as long as I'd known her, but sometimes she spoke about her late husband and son— both lost to a bus bombing in Sri Lanka. Was hers an arranged marriage? Had she met her husband on a sticky summer night like this one?

"Soon it'll be your turn," she said.

"I won't get married." I spoke to my sketchbook. I'd never said it out loud, but the words had been forming in my head for years.

"Of course you will, dear."

My hand shook where I gripped the pencil. "I won't." Itching crept in from the corners of my eyes. "I'm not like Shyama. I can't."

Laila Aunty turned and looked at me, her eyes poring over my messy hair, my legs spread open on the wire hotel chair, the thin rainbow bracelet I'd taken to wearing.

"You'll grow out of it," she said.

"What if I don't?"

She looked back down at the people sliding through each other on the sidewalk. "You will."

~

It took Amma and Laila Aunty over an hour to dress Shyama for the big night. They matched jewelry from old English biscuit tins stuffed into the bottoms of their purses. They fought over whether she should wear a saree or a churidar.

"A saree is just too old fashioned," Laila Aunty said. She wouldn't budge, so Shyama wore a churidar.

Amma draped a necklace on Shyama's neck, placed gold bangles and earrings on the counter. No way those earrings were going to fit. Shyama's ear holes were punched at a mall kiosk with a piercing gun—no thicker than a sewing needle. Indian earrings had heavy stems that gradually weighed down women's earlobes.

Amma held out a tube of moisturizer. "Try some cream."

She slathered lotion on Shyama's lobes and hands. While Shyama squeezed the bangles over her knuckles and onto her wrists, Amma pushed a too-thick stem against Shyama's piercing, which stretched against the pressure. Her ears flushed purple. With a pop, the stem slid in. Amma did the same to the other ear, while Laila Aunty wiped up bits of blood off Shyama's lobes and neck.

I dressed quietly in the churidar they gave me. Thankfully no one noticed me or fussed.

~

As we drove toward Rajesh's parents' house, Shyama clicked more and more manically at her phone.

Amma turned around in her seat. "Put that away. Don't bring it into the house."

Shyama deleted Dave's texts before turning off her phone and stowing it in the back of the driver's seat.

We neared the outskirts of Toronto and high rises gave way to row houses and then to new development neighborhoods with large homes on small plots. Lawns manicured green, flower boxes trimmed, decks tidy. And plenty of white people everywhere on the sidewalks, walking their dogs, jogging. After a few days of only seeing brown skin, I noticed them more than usual. I wondered if they had any idea that arranged marriages were taking place under their noses, that young men and women were marrying people they didn't know.

Appa pulled into a driveway at the end of a cul-de-sac and turned off the car. For a moment no one moved, and then with a "Here we go," Amma opened her door and stepped out. Shyama shivered in her sleeveless churidar. I was glad to have worn long sleeves. Steep steps led to the door, squeezed in between two houses on either side as if the front of the house was just too large for the space.

"Stand up straight," Amma said. She rang the doorbell.

Shyama pulled her shoulders back. Laila Aunty adjusted her clothes. The door opened and a high-school-aged girl grinned at us with braces.

"Please come in," she said so quietly that even Amma leaned forward to hear. She led us to the living room from the foyer. Rajesh's father shook hands with Appa. Amma and Laila Aunty smiled and nodded at Rajesh's mother. There was a lot of nodding all around. Rajesh avoided Shyama's eyes but greeted everyone else.

We took our seats. The plastic covering on the sofa crinkled as we sat down. Shyama twirled a piece of her hair around and around her finger.

"Your parents said you're doing your degree in biochemistry," Rajesh's father said to Shyama. He was a short, stout man with watery eyes and a bald head.

His wife looked shrunken in on herself, her skin saggy like

Grandmother's. Rajesh's sister sat with her eyes on the floor. Through her tissue-thin shirt, I could see the faint outline of her shoulders.

"What are you going to do after graduation?"

Everyone looked at Shyama but she didn't answer.

"She is concentrating on school right now," Amma said. "Shyama wants to take some time after college to do her writing and things."

"She's a good writer," Appa said. "She's always writing these stories about our culture."

"Lucky for you then. My son doesn't need his wife to work, so you can do your writing."

"She can teach classes," Amma said.

Shyama stared at the carpet. I held a cushion against my stomach and did the same. I was good at being quiet, but Shyama never was. Until now. In between the beige carpet strands, dark ones grew like weeds. Thick navy curtains hung over the windows. Potted plants hung in seashell planters. Each wall held pictures of Rajesh and his sister at various ages.

"Don't worry, Shyama. My son doesn't know yet how to cook but he's a good learner."

The parents laughed. Rajesh looked at Shyama but when she looked back, he turned away.

"Why don't we let the two of them go and talk?"

"I want to take a drive," Rajesh said.

He led Shyama out to the car while the parents continued to talk in the living room. Rajesh's mother got up to make tea.

Amma pushed me by the shoulders toward Rajesh's sister. "Why don't you go talk with her? She's your age."

I got up and sat on a hard dining chair next to Rajesh's sister.

She smiled shyly and looked at the floor again. She had a dark spot on her cheek that moved when she smiled.

"Do you like Tamil movies?" she asked.

"Some."

"I like Rajnikanth movies."

She sounded like Nisha, though I could never tell if Nisha actually liked the movies or if she said it because it made her parents happy.

Rajesh's sister was called to help serve the tea. She bent down in front of me and held out a silver tray of teacups and suddenly I felt like the groom in a Tamil movie meeting the bride for the first time—this scene so iconic it's in almost every Tamil film.

The parents talked more and more nervously as time went on and Shyama hadn't returned with Rajesh. By the time they came back, Amma and Appa had schooled their anxiety into fake smiles.

Amma waited until we were back in the car and had pulled out of the driveway. She turned around from the front seat.

"Well?"

Shyama turned on her phone. Its screen lit her face in blue.

"He seems like a nice boy, no?" Laila Aunty said.

"Very good family."

There were five texts from Dave.

"You like him, no?"

"Not really," Shyama said.

"What is that," Amma said, "not really?"

"I mean, I don't like him."

"Why not?"

"I just don't."

"What do you not like? He's a good boy."

"There just wasn't any chemistry."

"Chemistry?" Amma's voice rose in pitch and volume with each word. "Chemistry? What does that have to do with it?"

"There just weren't—you know—any sparks."

"Sparks. So now you want sparks. Sparks cause fires."

Shyama looked down at her phone and read the texts. *I miss you. You're the most beautiful girl I've ever met. We train 10 hours a day and every minute I think about you.*

"The chemistry will come with time," Laila Aunty said.

Amma turned to Appa, who was silent. Was he thinking about Laila Aunty, about the divorce papers he knew he was going to file?

"Your daughter is a fool," Amma said.

Shyama flies into town with her husband Rajesh and their one-year-old son Varun for Nisha's engagement ceremony. Appa and I pick them up from the airport. Shyama's hair jumps around her plump face like electricity. She hasn't started to show yet, but her cheeks are a little rounder than they'd been between pregnancies. Varun rides on her hip, his smooth face on her shoulder. Rajesh lags behind them as they walk out of the glass security doors, rolling a green flowered suitcase behind him.

Shyama was never the pretty one. She was the nice one, the one who made our parents happy. She convinced a five-year-old me to take dance class, pushed me into practicing when my legs hurt, attended every single one of my performances up until she went to college.

But now, the energy seems sucked out of her. She looks small in the open air beside the building's steel columns. She smiles when she sees us, but even that seems strained. I can't tell if Rajesh smiles or not—his skin is so dark that I can only tell from a distance when he shows his teeth. Varun turns and presses his face further into Shyama's shoulder. I hold out my arms to him but he clings on tighter.

"He'll come around after he gets used to you again."

Appa leads us through the airport toward central parking, always at the helm. Of course, he drives home. Rajesh rides in the front seat because he's a man.

I entertain Varun while Shyama snores with her head on the window. Varun smells like baby powder when I kiss his temples. At least Grandmother will be happy now that there's a baby in the house. Maybe she'll stop sitting outside.

"Are you sure you want to stay there?" Appa asks as he takes the exit to Winchester. His voice is hard around the edges. Appa offered to have them at his house but Shyama chose to stay with Amma.

Rajesh turns around in his seat for help from Shyama, who's sleeping. He turns back and makes a noncommittal grunt.

At Amma's house, Appa follows us inside and stands in the doorway, studiously brushing lint off the suitcases until Amma invites him inside for dinner.

Amma carries Varun around, kissing his cheeks and laughing while Grandmother watches from her folding chair. Bright toys litter the meticulously-scrubbed floor. Appa sits at the kitchen table with Rajesh and watches, the two of them slowly sipping the whiskey that Rajesh bought at the dutyfree. Everyone smiles too big.

I help Shyama unpack. I set up the air mattress pump and

leave it to fill while Shyama puts clothes into neat piles in the dresser drawers that Amma has cleaned out. Sleep casts deep shadows on her eyes, the skin around them almost purple. I'm not used to seeing her face so bare and tired.

"How long have you been here?" She carefully folds baby clothes in the topmost drawer.

"A month or so." Nisha's visits, Grandmother's slow mania, everything blurs together.

She turns around and puts her fists on her hips, looking so much like Amma that a chuckle tries to bubble up in my throat.

"You haven't seen Kris in a month?"

"He came for Nisha's party."

She narrows her eyes at me and doesn't move.

"I miss him. It's hard being away from him."

She stares at me for a few more seconds, then sighs heavily and picks up some of Rajesh's underwear from her suitcase. "Sometimes I wonder about you two."

Shyama's always been observant, and unlike Amma she doesn't let facts like our marriage get in the way.

"Why did you do it?" I ask. "Why did you marry Rajesh?"

She stuffs a pile of underwear into the dresser. "I don't regret it." She sounds like she believes it. "Rajesh is everything I could've asked for in a husband."

"You didn't like him when you met him. You liked Dave."

She turns around and hushes me. Her eyes linger on the doorway. She unzips another suitcase. "Dave was nice. But we always had problems. It wasn't worth the fight. Once I gave Rajesh a chance, I was happy." She shakes out some blouses and puts them on hangers. When she catches my eye in the mirror, she looks away and stacks diapers into another drawer. "Hard to believe that Nisha's getting married. Then again, it's hard to believe that you got married—how long ago was it?"

"Four years."

"Four years. God, I feel old."

She looks old. Gray creeps into her hair, streaking the blackness like lightning. She is starting to take on the saggy thickness of Amma's skin. I like the look on her, but she probably hates it.

"How's the groom?" she asks. "Have you met him?"

"I saw a picture."

She empties the suitcase and turns it upside down over the trashcan. "And?" She bounces it up and down until a couple of crumbs fall out.

"He's no Kris."

She puts down the empty suitcase and heaves another one on top of the bed. "I thought Nisha would be able to do better than that, with her looks and all."

I pick at a loose thread on Amma's comforter. Unbidden, Nisha in her red wedding saree fills my brain. Nisha with real jasmines in her hair. Nisha with a thali. Nisha on her wedding night.

"What I wouldn't give for that girl's looks," Shyama says.

I snap the thread loose from the rest of the stitching and wind it around my finger until it bites into my skin. "She's very pretty," I say.

⁓

After a hurried and hushed call to Laila Aunty, Appa informs us that he's staying for dinner. He laughs through the food, loudly and more often than I've heard him laugh in months. He loves all of us, but Shyama has always been his favorite. When she left for college, he moped around the house and started working late and on the weekends. But during Shyama's visits home he would somehow find his weekends and nights free and would come home early with groceries to make her favorite foods. The divorce shattered their relationship. Shyama never forgave him, refusing to stay at his house, and taking Amma's side in all arguments.

Now Appa takes generous sips of his whiskey and smiles wide enough to show his teeth. He waxes political about the first debate of the election season. Obama's chances are dwindling, but Appa remains hopeful.

Rajesh nods mutely and stuffs his face with food. I wouldn't brag about my ability to eat with my hands, but I feel like a saint next to Rajesh, whose plate is surrounded with spilled food. He's one of those men who was hand-fed by his adoring grandmother well into adolescence. Will Nisha's husband be like that? Will Nisha cook for him?

"It's about time for Nisha," Amma says. "She was getting so old."

Appa and Rajesh talk about work. Rajesh is pissed about being passed up for a promotion. "You know," he says, brandishing a drumstick at us, "I bet if I was white those sons of bitches would promote me."

He says shit like this all the time, especially when he's been drinking. He's embarrassed by his thick accent and Sri Lankan degree, angry at his coworkers for not inviting him out to bars. He thinks he doesn't get promotions because his boss is racist. I think it's because he's shy around white people.

"You'll get a promotion," Appa says.

"I need it. We have to get that extra room done on the house. The city makes us take out so many permissions, you know. They hate to see us doing so well."

They don't need an extra room. But they're the kind of people who buy a Mercedes when the next-door neighbor buys a BMW.

Appa makes little noises of confirmation and the rest of us stay quiet. Shyama's lack of embarrassment makes me angry.

"You need that room," Appa says. He sucks down the rest of his drink and looks at Amma expectantly. When she doesn't look up or refill his glass, he sets it aside and goes back to his food.

~

Kris goes to a conference in Seattle and can't make it for Nisha's engagement. At least this time we won't fight about how much he's allowed to touch me. I won't have to drag his drunk ass home.

We go to the bank to get jewelry out of Amma's safe-deposit box. Rajesh drives Amma's Camry through the winding, narrow streets of Arlington. Inside the small room at the bank, with the long, cold metal safe-deposit box open on the counter, Amma, Shyama and I sort through the years of gold accumulation to find suitably modern enough pieces to wear to Nisha's engagement. Rajesh entertains his son outside.

Shyama chooses a small necklace with a grape-like cluster of black stones.

"That's much too small," Amma says. She pulls out a plastic pencil box and unfolds the old baby washcloth inside—I wonder if it's mine—faded from its pastel glory to a dingy white. Amma's wedding necklace lies inside, wrapped and carefully held onto the fabric with safety pins. Twenty-two karat gold, with white stones that look like diamonds but aren't. She unpins the necklace carefully and holds it up to my neck, draping it around my collar. Even though I got a similar, more expensive necklace from Appa, I still love Amma's. The gold is blackened at the corners where the links of the floral chain connect to each other. This necklace feels like it has history, even though Amma told me that the black means the gold is impure.

"Can I wear this one?" I ask. "You can wear mine."

Amma clucks her tongue. "This one is old-fashioned, for old ladies like me."

I take it off my neck and wrap it carefully back in the washcloth.

"You have strange taste, Lucky. You can wear it if you want."

I put the washcloth back in the pencil case and snap it shut.

"I just want to see a smile on your face." Amma unzips another jewelry case and collects a set of gold bangles on her finger. Two of them are Shyama's favorites, with little pearls embedded in the filigree.

I try to pick out the smallest earrings and a necklace large enough that it will lay flat instead of twisting. I hate fussing with things I'm wearing. Plus I have to wear my thali, and that's too thick to be comfortable. Amma's insistent on not skipping that part—the mark of a married woman is important.

Amma ordered sarees from India and Shyama got the blouses stitched in Toronto according to each of our measurements. I haven't even seen the saree I'm supposed to wear.

Shyama and Amma hold up various pieces of jewelry to themselves, trying to imagine the sarees and how they'll look.

They debate on this bangle or that, whether or not they should wear tikkas and what size their earrings should be. I try to busy myself with wrapping each necklace carefully back in its fabric scrap and sorting the ones we're taking from the ones we're leaving behind.

Tasha invites Nisha and me to a rugby game she's referereeing. Radcliffe vs. BU. At the game, Nisha spreads out a blanket on the wet stadium grass. She crawls onto it and pats the space next to her. Tasha waves at us from the field where the two teams are warming up. Nisha shivers in the cooling air, so I hold her around the waist. People mill around us, setting up lawn chairs and trying to keep track of toddlers who've just learned to run.

"How do you know Tasha?" I ask. The rugby girls seem like such an odd group for Nisha, but maybe she was different in college. Maybe she was out. We didn't talk much after high school, so maybe this was a part of Nisha's past I didn't know about.

Nisha smiles and watches the Radcliffe team jog around the pitch. "My first semester at Wellesley, I went crazy and thought I should try sports."

"So you picked rugby?"

"It wasn't so bad."

"You played?"

She raises an eyebrow. "Why? Am I too delicate in your eyes?"

"No." I say it too quickly.

"I played a semester. But practice started cutting into study time. I couldn't keep up." She rests a hand on my knee. "Plus Amma and Appa started asking about the bruises."

"I want to see you play." I wonder if her fiancé knows he's marrying a rugby player. If he could see her now, kissing my neck, smearing her sticky gloss all over my skin.

"I'll play next time," she says into my ear.

She spends the first half of the game running her fingers up and down my thigh, explaining the rules I don't understand.

At halftime Tasha walks with us to her car. We sit inside. She offers us a bottle of Sprite. "It's mostly vodka."

Nisha uncaps it. She takes a swig and grimaces. She passes it to me. For the first time in a long time I don't feel like drinking. But she holds it out so I take it. The mixture bites into my tongue and leaves a bitter aftertaste that stays in my nose.

Tasha refuses the bottle. "Later," she says. She sits backward in the driver's seat and watches the two of us. "Has Nisha told you she used to play?"

"It's not that big a deal," Nisha says.

"You were a solid player."

"I was an okay player."

"Remember the Brandeis game? When you tackled Lu and knocked her out?"

"I bumped her head with my shoulder by accident when we fell down."

"It was fucking badass. I wish you'd play with us more."

Nisha drinks some more from the Sprite bottle. I feel like I'm seeing her for the first time. When she leaves for the bathroom, Tasha smokes a cigarette and flicks the ashes out of the half-open window.

"I should quit," she says. "It's horrible for my game."

"Why did Nisha stop playing?" I ask.

Tasha lowers her voice. "I think her parents found out. It wasn't pretty. I keep trying to get her to come out to JP more. It can't be good for her to be stuck in the house with her parents all the time."

"They've always been strict." Nisha had an eight-o'clock bedtime all through high school. She wasn't allowed to wear shorts or skirts above her knees. The only time she could go out with her friends was when I was invited along.

⁓

During the second half of the game, Nisha and I walk around the edge of the pitch to stave off the cold. Neither of us have jackets. The cool air sinks into our skin and stays there.

She walks fast around the pitch. I lightly touch her elbow and she stops.

"Amma wants us to have a sangeet as part of the wedding," she says. "I'd have to perform a dance."

I thread my fingers through hers. "Will Deepak dance with you?"

She winds a hand around my neck. "I miss dancing with you."

"I can't dance at the sangeet with you."

Her eyes light up. "But you can dance with me now." She pulls me away from the pitch and down past a thicket of bushes.

The noise of the game dies into a muffle. Nisha sits down in a clearing that looks like it's designed for team meetings before games. She unzips her boots and takes them off. I untie my shoes and step out of them. She finds a song on her phone. She turns up the volume and leaves it in the grass.

"Ready?" She takes her position.

"What song?"

"Our song." She misses the first beat of the drum, but catches up quickly.

It's a routine we choreographed for the Boston Tamil Arts Festival. A two-person dance from a Rajnikanth movie about misplaced love and vengeance. Appropriate.

She remembers her parts well. I try to keep up. I'm not used to moving this way anymore, bending at the waist or curving with the violin notes. Nisha dances like she's never stopped. Barefoot in the grass, her face making all the right emotions to the lyrics. Her legs lift with the drums, leaping and dancing around me.

I'd played the male part, the object of the female dancer's affection, who had wanted a different girl instead, a girl too shy to dance in public. A good, modest servant girl who, in the music video, edged around the walls of the dance floor casting coy glances at the hero.

Nisha mouths the lyrics to me, dancing around and around, circling. *You keep following me, without asking what I want.* But she wants this. *Don't you want to be the one that catches the flowers that fall from my hair?*

At the end of the song, the female dancer kisses the hero in front of his family, raising a scandal that moves the plot forward. In our version for the arts festival, Nisha kissed my cheek at the end and walked off the stage. As I stood there pretending to be stunned, the curtain dropped. Fade to black.

I start to remember the movement. I get better as the song progresses, and by the end I'm dancing without watching Nisha for cues. The drums beat louder, and Nisha slows her movement. She stops dancing and circles me. When the song ends she kisses me on the mouth, pulls me down into the grass, and slides my hand up her leg.

"What if someone sees?" I say. But there's no one around. Cheering floats through the bushes from the game.

She's wiry and dark under me. Her hair glints with the coppery sky and snakes through the grass in black coils. She throws back her head and mutters to me in Tamil, half-words that scratch and bite at my skin and make me press up against her leg, press press press until I cry into her shoulder and she holds me and kisses me softly on the cheek.

⁓

For a whole three hours during the game I haven't checked my phone, and there are five texts from Amma wondering where I am. Nisha has three missed calls.

"They're going to be so mad," she says. She hurriedly pulls on her boots. She swings her purse over her shoulder and smoothes down her dress. "Ready?"

"Why do they want you home?"

"They always want me home."

"Is that why you stopped dancing? And playing rugby?"

She takes a step toward the field. "They were really mad about the rugby." She digs up a rock on the ground, rolls her foot on top of it. "But the dancing—it just wasn't the same with you gone. Plus they said I was too old."

I touch her waist and she relaxes against me. "You still dance like you used to. Puts me to shame."

She closes her eyes against the breeze. Her head falls on my shoulder. "I miss you."

"I'm right here."

"After—when I'm—you know."

My feet step away from her and toward the field. I forgot, just for a moment. Misplaced affection. But my heart still beats faster when she grabs my hand and holds it all the way to the field. I still kiss her back when she leans over in the car on the way home. I still tell her I want to see her play rugby.

Nisha wants me to help her dress for her engagement ceremony, which means sitting in the room and watching a
makeup artist do her face. She meets me in front of her parents'
house. The driveway is so full with cars that they spill onto the
side of the street and in front of mailboxes. Her hair falls wet
and stringy around her face. She pushes me inside.

The hollow wood floors echo with brown people talking over
each other. Nisha's parents and extended family cluster around
the kitchen island drinking tea. They aren't dressed yet, but the
women are already wearing their gold jewelry.

Nisha pulls me up the stairs, past the walls crowded with
JC Penney family portraits. The stairwell seems to tilt into
the middle as if weighed down by the clutter. We climb past the
massive picture of a twelve-year-old Nisha holding a lit
bronze lamp at her puberty ceremony, her hair done up

with purple carnations that match her lipstick—that was the first time I'd ever seen her in a saree or wearing makeup, and I thought she looked like a movie star. Nisha's room is exactly as I remember it. She's never decorated it beyond the two framed photos of herself as a baby and the stuffed animals twined into the curls of her wrought-iron bed. A box fan hums from her dresser.

"The makeup lady's on her way." She sits on the edge of the bed. Six yards of sherbet-orange silk ripples next to her. The afternoon light bleaches the waves where they crest. Gold embroidery shines like fish in the thread.

She stands up, slips off her shirt and threads her arms through the saree blouse. "Can you help?"

I hook the back of her blouse together and tie the strings. The neck is cut deep, exposing her spine. She bends back. My fingers brush her skin.

"I can't believe this is happening," she says. She steps out of her jeans and ties the cotton underskirt around her waist. Her smile shows her whitened teeth, long and evenly spaced thanks to years of braces. She has her blue contacts in, the ones that make her eyes look glassy like a doll's.

"It's good to see you excited," I say. I hope I don't sound bitter. "Are Jesse and Tasha coming today?"

"You should be careful around them." She walks to the small wooden vanity next to her bed and sits down on its upholstered stool. She smiles and unsmiles in the mirror like she's practicing. She can smile with her eyes even when she doesn't mean it. "They could get you into trouble, if your mother sees. I know your parents aren't as strict, but I still doubt your mother would be happy if she knew."

The door opens and a woman I don't know peeks her head

in. Her wide face and small, upturned eyes would be friendly if it wasn't for the heavy makeup she wears.

"Gauri Aunty," Nisha says. "I'm ready."

The drape of Gauri Aunty's churidar hides her curves, but she doesn't look much older than us. She hauls in a large silver makeup train case.

"Can you get the rest?" She points to the door.

I bring in the two plastic totes just outside the door.

Gauri Aunty combs through Nisha's hair. "Can you plug in the curling iron and straightener?"

Both the iron and straightener are bright pink. I plug them in behind the bed and let them heat up. Nisha's saree runs like water under my fingers.

Gauri Aunty straightens and then curls Nisha's hair. She pins it into a high bun, pulls out three roses from the tiniest cooler I've ever seen, and attaches them at the base of Nisha's neck.

I text Kris: *Nisha's getting all dolled up for the engagement. You, too?*

Fuck no.

Are you helping her get dressed? Sexy time?

I turn the phone off and stuff it back in my pocket.

Gauri Aunty rolls out a makeup brush holder and spreads it on the vanity like a painter would. She unclamps the train case and pulls out drawers of little vials, takes Nisha's face in hand, spreads this and that on her face, brushes puffed up with powder, shimmering shadows on her eyelids, dark liner around her eyes, a deep stain on her lips. Nisha stands up, and Gauri Aunty helps wrap her saree, pinning it in places where she normally would have tucked the fabric into the petticoat, going for the thinnest silhouette possible.

I'm getting twitchy. I wish I'd brought my sketchbook. I would've drawn Nisha getting painted. Instead I drum on my thighs and read the labels on the makeup. Deep Throat, Virgin, Sin, Pop My Cherry, Orgasm. Who names this stuff?

Gauri Aunty jerks her head toward me. "Do you want me to do her, too?"

Nisha looks at me. She's unrecognizable with all the makeup. She raises her eyebrows like she wants an answer.

"I don't think so," I say.

"Do her makeup," Nisha says.

Gauri Aunty pins jewelry into Nisha's hair, stacks necklaces on her chest. I know how Nisha feels, so many bobby pins that your head is twice its weight, so much makeup that it's like looking out of a mask, jewelry on every part of you so that you can't even move. I had to endure it for my wedding. Then again, it's Nisha. She probably enjoys the feeling. She looks beautiful enough to make it worth it.

Nisha sits stiffly on the bed and Gauri Aunty turns to me.

"Will this take long?" I say. It's nearly noon and Nisha still has a one-hour photo session before the ceremony.

"Take your time," Nisha says.

Gauri Aunty makes me sit with my back to the mirror as she straightens my hair and puts makeup on my face. Nisha snaps a picture on her phone. When I try to take it away, she holds it beyond my reach and tells me she's posting it online.

⌒

The photos take forever. I'm still in my jeans and T-shirt so I help the thick-spectacled, pushy-voiced photographer set up a portable studio in the den. Nisha sits a full head height below Deepak, even though she's not much shorter than him. Photo: Nisha with her head on his shoulder. Photo: her hand lies delicately in his. Photo: she looks up at him, in profile. Zoom in on her earrings, on her eyes, on the roses in her hair.

"Smile, smile." The photographer poses them like dolls. "No, Deepak. You don't smile. Nisha, smile." Nisha has always been a good actress.

She talks to me throughout the shoot. Deepak watches her and wipes sweat from his forehead with a cotton handkerchief. I watch her, too, her mouth and two perfect rows of teeth, whitened and gleaming under the bright lights, framed by maroon lips. Photo: Deepak lifts her face with a finger under her chin. Photo: she looks up at him adoringly. Photo: pitiful freak watching the girl she loves get married. Photo: two adoring best friends laughing about boys. Photo: the bride looks sad when she thinks no one is looking. Photo: composed, scripted. The real story lies in between the pigments.

Nisha's parents rent out the first floor of a gilded, carpeted hotel. White linens blanket everything like a fine dusting of snow. Giant crystal chandeliers twinkle from the arched ceilings. By the time I get there, the guests have already started to arrive, swishing their saree pleats around their glittery stilettos. It makes me think of Bollywood movies, of curvy, milk-skinned heroines and men who never take no for an answer.

My flask lies warm and full on my skin, tucked into the waistband of my saree.

I find Jesse and Tasha milling around near the mango lassi table, dressed in slacks and bow ties and looking both enthralled and confused. They smile when they see me.

"You look nice. I think we're underdressed." Tasha wipes at her suit vest and fixes her polka-dot pocket square.

"I'm paying for it. This saree is itchy as hell. And I have lipstick on." At least Kris isn't here to hold me tight to his side, to flirt with me when he thinks everyone is watching. I wonder if Tasha and Jesse even know I'm married.

Amma and Grandmother arrive just in time for the ceremony. Amma doesn't come to most Sri Lankan functions. She says she likes to avoid the gossip—she's only one of four divorced women in the Boston Tamil community, so gossip trails after her. She usually pretends to be sick, or says she has to work. When she can't get out of important functions, she comes late and leaves early and tries not to talk to many people.

She looks in my direction and I turn away. She's probably already accounted for how many people have noticed me standing with Jesse and Tasha. American friends are okay, but not if they wear men's clothes. I'm surprised Nisha even invited them.

"How are you handling all this?" Jesse asks.

I don't like her look of pity. I take a glass of mango lassi so I have something to hold onto.

"Leave her alone," Tasha says.

"This isn't fair," Jesse says. "You know that."

People turn around to look.

"This is Nisha's choice," Tasha whispers.

"I can't believe she'd choose this. Not Nisha."

"I'm fine," I say. "Seriously." They both look skeptical. "I brought a flask."

Tasha snorts into her lassi.

"You brought a flask to an engagement?"

"Yes, I fucking brought a flask. Every man here brought a flask to this engagement. Do you want some or not?"

We find an unused room and pass the flask around. I take more than my share. It's my fucking flask. We wander over to the official drink table with the sodas and pour some for ourselves. The whiskey works its way through my system. The drink chills my fingers. I hold the plastic cup to my forehead and let the cool seep in. Nisha won't want Gauri Aunty's makeup melting off my face before the ceremony even starts.

"Lucky!"

Laila Aunty's thin frame pushes someone aside to come stand next to me. Her smile is too bright, her makeup too vivid. "These are your friends?" She looks from me to Jesse to Tasha, her smile now permanently marring her face.

I introduce them. "They're Nisha's friends."

Laila Aunty asks Jesse and Tasha what they do, where they live, what they studied in school. She nods back and forth, her smile never wavering from her face. When she leaves, Tasha elbows me.

"Are we only Nisha's friends?"

The lights dim before I can answer, and the ceremony starts. Deepak's parents and Nisha's parents gather around a covered table set up at one end of the ballroom. A three-tier cream cake stands on one end, and a man in a traditional veshti sarong stands at the other. The unbleached white cotton of his veshti and kurta shirt looks crisp and starched against his dark skin. He places a marriage certificate in front of him, in between six trays covered with gold and red fabric.

Nisha and Deepak walk up the aisle in the middle of the room. Her saree twirls around her as she walks, the embroidered stones splitting light like shattered glass. In person, Deepak looks even more puffed up with air.

When the man at the table nods, Nisha's parents give Deepak's parents three silver trays: one with the sherwani that Deepak will wear for the wedding and the suit that he'll wear for the reception, one with flowers and fruits, and one with betel leaves, areca nuts, sandalwood paste, and other things I can't even name. Deepak's parents give three trays: one with Nisha's wedding and reception sarees, one with lipstick, eyeliners, and the gold thali kodi, and one with the same assortment of nuts and spices.

After the exchange, the man at the table clears his throat and speaks in Tamil. "This is the engagement of Deepak and Nisha. Their parents have given their blessings with the exchange of gifts. Do you, Deepak, agree to this marriage?"

Deepak holds his own wrist and nods.

I translate quietly for Tasha and Jesse.

"Isn't it rude to talk?" Tasha asks.

"Not at a brown function." I'm thankful for the whiskey inside my system. It plants my feet to the floor and keeps me steady. Everything blurs.

"I thought this was an engagement," Tasha says.

"Sri Lankan engagements mean signing the marriage license."

"Nisha, do you agree to this marriage?" the man asks.

Tasha whispers in my ear. "So are you two still fucking?"

"Yes," Nisha says.

The man produces two rings in a red velvet case and holds them out. Deepak takes one and puts it on Nisha's finger. Nisha puts the other on Deepak's. The saree creeps up Nisha's back as she bends down to sign the marriage license.

I step away from Tasha. I know what Amma will say if she sees. I shake my head and hope that Tasha will take that as an answer. My fingertips are expanding at the edges from all the heat in the room.

Dinner is served buffet style. I follow Tasha and Jesse through the line, explaining the dishes as best as I can. Their presence keeps most of the older people away and for that I'm grateful. No one asking me when I'm going to have a kid, when I'm going to become one of them.

Nisha comes and sits with us while we eat at a table by ourselves. Amma's disappeared but Laila Aunty smiles at us in between bites from a table nearby.

"I'm so tired," Nisha says. She carefully takes a bite of rice and lentils from her spoon using only her teeth. Her face is shiny with sweat.

Jesse stares at her plate. She's piled on everything from the buffet, and her plate's so full that she can't mix the curries with the rice. Tasha's spoon is a blur with the speed of her eating. Nisha's silence grates at me. She wants me to say something.

"It was great," I say. "You looked great."

Nisha squeezes my knee underneath the table and takes another bite from her spoon.

"Thanks for coming," she says to Tasha and Jesse.

"Wouldn't miss it." Jesse digs her spoon directly into the middle of her pile and starts eating.

Tasha says nothing.

Nisha smiles and walks away with her plate.

"I should've brought a bigger flask," I say.

"We're going to the bars after this," Tasha says. "You should come."

"I'm in a saree."

"And?"

And Amma won't let me go. I'm sure of it. It's nine already, and by the time we finish eating and get ready to leave, it'll be ten. Then there's getting to the club in Boston, by car and T. We wouldn't be done until two or three in the morning. Way past my curfew.

"You can stay over at the rugby house," Tasha says.

"I have to ask my mom."

If they think that's weird, they keep it to themselves. Amma's cornered near the cake table by Laila Aunty. Perfect. Either she'll say yes, to prove to Laila Aunty that she's the kind of parent who trusts her kid, or she'll say no, to prove to Laila Aunty that she isn't the kind of parent who will neglect the dangers of the night scene. Each would result in a fight.

I walk over like I want a slice of cake. Amma pretends not to see me, but Laila Aunty lets out a high-pitched "Lucky!" and puts an arm around my shoulders. Amma's pinched face turns toward me.

"Amma, my friends are asking if I want to go to Boston with them."

"Go to Boston? Why?"

"We're going to go dancing."

"When?"

"Now. I'll stay over at their house and come back in the morning."

Her nostrils quiver and flare.

"Oh, let her go," Laila Aunty says. "She's a grown up."

Amma takes in a breath of air that fills up her chest. Her face crumples. I try not to smile, but I've won.

⌐

Tasha's car slices through the streetlights on our way inbound, Chris Pureka's eerie low voice winding through the speakers and vibrating in my ribcage. I melt into the cracked vinyl backseat. Tasha and Jesse's conversation mixes in with the music. My fingers are still jittery with cold. I close my eyes.

We weave through the inky night, moving along a river of headlights, the city winking with the light of a million bulbs. I wish Nisha was sitting beside me, holding my hand the way that she does only around the rugby girls, Nisha in her engagement saree, the silk fabric folding into orange waves, gold glittering like fish in the sea. The whiskey has carved me empty.

Cool air streams inside the half-open windows of Tasha's car, the salt of the sea still riding on the wind, splashing against the mask of makeup on my face. Buildings swim past us and we're riding the wind, too, us and the salt of the sea, hurtling toward the city on a night that isn't special and doesn't matter, except that it does and I want the car to slide, to give up its traction on the asphalt and fly faster until our skin melts away and we are free.

⌐

At Machine, Tasha holds a ten-dollar bill in between her fingers and leans against the bar. She doesn't tilt her hips or stick out her butt the way Nisha does. The club expands like a cave, the darkness thick between the breaks of light. Tasha shouts drink orders into the bartender's ear and lays down more bills. "I got this round," she yells over the music.

I stuff my money back in my purse, wishing I'd left it in the car. I pull up my saree and pin it so that it doesn't fall over my arm. Tasha gives me a Sam Adams, raises hers in a toast, and tips her head back to drink. I let the cold beer rush into my mouth and fall down my throat. If only it could wash away the image of Nisha bending down to sign her marriage certificate, skin stretched tight over her lower back, the room too hot and I can't breathe.

Tasha hooks an arm around mine and pulls me toward the dance floor. I take another sip of beer and let myself be dragged. She squeezes us into an opening in the crowd of people, many of whom no longer have their shirts on, their chests and backs gleaming with sweat and glitter. The crowd keeps pushing us closer. I could grab her hip, pull it to me, push my face into the crook of her neck, breathe in the smell of her. I reach out. My fingers close on the rough material of her slacks. Over her shoulder, one shirtless girl pushes another one up against the wall. Tasha moves closer. She smells like leaves. Her breath skims my ear, along the skin of my collar, slips into the fabric of my saree and down my back. She feels solid. She comes forward, slowly slowly and closer closer and kisses my neck. But Nisha's face is stitched into the backs of my eyelids and I move away.

I push back against the crowd of dancers, turn away from

Tasha. My phone buzzes in my purse. A text from Nisha: *You left early.*

Went out with Tasha and Jesse.

I wanted you to be my witness for the marriage license.

Sorry.

Whatever.

I said I'm sorry. I didn't know.

I push my way off the dance floor, toward the bar. Jesse is standing next to a poster calling for dancers at the Mason Jar.

Tasha follows me. "I'm sorry for what happened back there." She puts her empty beer bottle on the bar and doesn't look me in the eye.

I drain the last of the beer and put my bottle next to hers. "I'm married."

"Oh."

I expect questions, but she doesn't ask them until later, when we're sitting on the deck of the rugby house and she's smoking her cigarette and tapping the ashes into an empty beer bottle with the label ripped off.

"You're married." She stuffs her free hand in her pocket and looks out into the street. The wind swoops in cold through the metal railings of the deck. The peeling white paint glows in the moonlight. Voices shout at a party down the street.

"Married to a guy?" she asks.

"His name's Kris."

"So you and Nisha?"

"Nisha's engaged."

"Yeah, but don't you have an arrangement? With your husband."

A couple of college kids run down the street, hooting and

pumping their fists into the air. She watches them until they turn the corner at the bottom of the hill. The air drips with dying roses.

"Kris is gay. We aren't together."

"So Nisha—"

"Nisha's engaged."

Tasha shivers and wraps her arms around herself. "Is this what you want?"

I wish I had a cigarette to put off answering. "What I want doesn't matter. Not to her."

I sleep in the living room under the tie-dyed quilt. Tasha sits on the couch and talks to me until I fall asleep, and when I wake up she's spread out flat, her head thrown back on a fuzzy orange pillow, her arm over her eyes, mouth hanging open. She makes me a breakfast that we eat out on the deck so that she can smoke. Birds sing unseen in bushes that haven't yet shed their leaves.

"Don't you want to do something?" she says.

I poke at my rapidly-cooling scrambled eggs. "Like what?"

She flicks her cigarette so hard that the lit end flies into the empty flowerbed. She waves her arms around. "How can you just sit there and pretend to accept this?"

She doesn't get it. She lives in a world of polyamory and multi-lover households, where marriage means whatever you want it to mean. But Nisha's marriage is real, and outside of stolen kisses at parties and dates masquerading as day trips to outlet malls, we will have nothing.

Tasha picks up a piece of scrambled egg from my plate and nibbles on it.

"This is what I want," I say. I can't tell if it's a lie. "I can't mess up my life. I worked too hard." I lied too much.

She listens in silence, eats another piece of egg from my plate, and opens the door to go inside. "How is living in pain not already messed up?" she says.

Amma opens the door when Tasha drops me off, and looks me up and down in my borrowed gym shorts and Patriots shirt. She looks out toward the dead-end street, where Tasha is turning her car around. "Is that a boy or a girl?"

I step inside the door and close it. "That's Tasha. She was at the engagement."

"Good. I got scared it was a boy."

Amma's in full cooking mode, three pans steaming on the range top and cutting board full of finely chopped onions, peppers, and tomatoes each in their own little pile.

"Grandmother has been asking for you." She stirs each of the pots on the stove. She dips a wooden spoon in one, taps the liquid onto her palm, and licks it. "Hand me the salt."

I take the salt from the counter and give it to her.

Amma sprinkles it over the bean curry and stirs. "She's out on the deck again. Do you know why she sits out there?"

"No." I go into the living room, open the glass doors and step outside. Grandmother sits on her folding chair, wrapped in her winter coat, thick wool socks and flip-flops.

"Vidya," she says. "You turned into a boy. You can't have a baby if you're a boy."

"It's me, Lucky." I put a palm to Grandmother's forehead. It isn't any warmer or colder than it should be.

She takes my hand in both of hers. "You should have a baby. Krishna wants a baby." She rubs my knuckles and shakes a cough from her lips.

I pull from her grasp. She has moments of lucidity, but this is the first time she's remembered Kris's name in years. I go back inside.

Amma rolls leaves of cabbage into tight circles and slices them. "What did she want?"

"She wants me to have a baby."

"Good. You need to start a family. You're getting older, Lucky. You can't just run around like a teenager anymore. You have to have responsibilities." She throws the sliced cabbage into a glass dish full of water. "You don't know how happy it will make you when you have a family."

This is the same thing she said when she wanted me to get married, before Kris and I came up with our plan. Same speech: I didn't realize how unhappy I was and I couldn't even guess at the boundless happiness a marriage could give. Shyama was held up as the example.

"We want to see a grandchild before we die," she says.

She already has a grandchild, but I don't have energy for the hysterics right now. I sit and listen and don't talk back. She turns off two of the burners and wipes at her eyes. I should be moved by this, the sight of my mother in distress, but I feel nothing. Her body slumps over her curries.

ESCAPING FATE

When I close my eyes I can feel the lights of Machine floating around me like dust, my body alive with movement. I dream about it at night. The need to move is like an itch under my skin.

I think about the ad for the Mason Jar that hung at Machine, when I sit in the living room and paint on my laptop, when I shower, when I lay awake in bed—the rail-thin dancer on the ad, the blocky colors of the poster.

I go to the auditions and sit outside in the car for an hour. Once or twice I try to get out and join the jerky stream of women suctioned into spandex skirts and plunging blouses. Always try new things, right? I should've worn something sexier than brown corduroys and a U2 shirt, something that would get their blood pumping. The security guard watches me in the car. I hold onto the steering wheel. I pretend to read a book. I rummage in the glove box to pass the time.

Amma calls. "Where are you?"

"I'm on my way home."

"I've been worried."

I've only been gone an hour. "I'll be there soon."

She's waiting at the kitchen island when I come home. Heated up leftovers lie spread out on the counter.

"Where were you?"

"Picking up some things from the store."

⌒

I start practicing when Amma's at work and Grandmother is sitting out on the deck. I'm woefully out of shape. I drag the floor-length mirrors from the bathroom and guest bedroom into Amma's room and set them up side by side against the armoire. My reflection looks unsure. I could stand to lose a few pounds.

I move, thick and unpracticed, my feet already hurting, my knees squeaky every time I put weight on them, my arms trembling when I hold them in position, my thighs tired of the constant tension. I relearn the mudras with my hands. I used to be able to run through the set without thinking, but now my fingers freeze and stumble over gestures. Arm movements are jerkier, sloppier, but my muscles still know how to push through the ache in my shoulders. I can't move my feet the way I used to, can't jump and slap the ground to the beat. I wish Nisha were here to dance with me. Next to her, I can be invisible.

Lasyam, the goddess Parvati's graceful, fluid melody of feminine energy. Tandavam, Shiva's masculine cosmic dance—strong, staccato, mountainous. Bharatanatyam, a combination of the two styles, is inherently androgynous. In the mirror I watch my head and eyes. In Bharatanatyam even the eyes move to the beat, each part of the body independent from the rest. My body still knows the songs.

I find a box of my old dance costumes in the basement and lay them out on Amma's bed. The thin silk smells like my sweat, infused from many recitals. I arrange and rearrange the pleats that connect the two legs, the material shot through with so much embroidery that the original color is barely visible. I try on the jewelry, drape the headpiece on my parted hair, straighten out the crooked jewels that hang down over my forehead, tie the black shoestrings behind my head, pin the small sun and moon pieces to either side of my hair part, clip the fake nose ring on, and stack three necklaces on top of my T-shirt. Nisha used to help me dress for performances and draw fake henna on my hands using a red Sharpie.

I look in the mirror and expect to see myself at eighteen, a clone of the picture downstairs on Amma's photo wall. But all I see is me.

Nisha invites me to a beach in Gloucester with the rugby girls. We stop in town to buy beer and snacks. The air smells like fish and salt.

"This town smells like Sri Lanka," I say. Back when we used to visit, back when my family was still whole. We flew back tanned and complicated, split between missing the blue warmth and grateful to leave all the soldiers behind.

Nisha scrunches up her nose and picks out a bag of Tostitos. "It does. But no one knows us here." She steps closer to me and puts the chip bag in the basket I'm holding. When she kisses me, her lips taste like fake strawberries.

"I love you," she says. She doesn't look at me.

~

The beach is bare and long during low tide. Fog rolls over the sand and obscures the ocean from view. People camp out under colorful umbrellas, in between the shaggy brush. We set up camp on an abandoned patch of sand. Nearby, a flock of seagulls attacks food left out by a family gone swimming.

Nisha sits next to me on a beach towel wearing only her swimsuit. Jesse and Tasha dig out beers and snacks. Jesse's arms look enormous in the tank top she wears. Every time she moves her biceps, the muscles change.

She catches me looking and flexes her arm. "Want to feel?"

I poke the hard bicep. I need to do more push-ups.

Nisha kisses me on the neck. "I like your arms the way they are," she says into my ear.

The seagulls descend on the camp next to us. Jesse and Tasha run to chase them away.

Nisha turns her back and pulls her hair to one side. "Could you retie this for me?"

I unknot her bikini, tie the strings tighter. She turns around and puts her fingers on my cheek. I look at her eyes through her sunglasses.

"Don't look so sad," she says. "He's as good as any guy I could find myself."

Tasha flaps her arms at the seagulls while Jesse puts away the family's food in bags and coolers.

"Have you dated either of them?"

"I dated Jesse in college. But that was ages ago. I was a different person. I thought I could be like them."

A seagull waddles toward us. Tasha and Jesse chase it away on their way back to our camp.

"Why can't you be like them?" I ask.

She draws circles in the sand. "We're not like them. We have to think about our families. If we lived like them, we'd lose everything."

I feel sick with chips and beer. My skin sticks with humidity.

Nisha pushes her fingers down and buries her hand. "I don't want to spend my life fighting a war I can't win."

I need to feel something more solid than air around me. "Let's swim." I stand up and say it again, louder so the others can hear. I walk toward the ocean. The others follow. It's not a warm day. Thorny seaweed and sharp cracked seashells dot the sand. The first cold steps take effort, but I push forward slowly. The water engulfs my feet and creeps upward with each wave, each step.

Tasha stops with the water up to her knees. "The tide is coming in."

Nisha walks by my side, her skin raised in goose bumps. "That's it, Tasha? That's how tough you are?"

Tasha scowls and marches forward.

I can't feel my legs from the cold. Nisha smiles at me and lets go of my hand.

I keep walking until the water moves around me like air. Waves pick me up as they pass. I dive into them, let the salt into my mouth. The cold soaks into my scalp. People must drown out here, pulled in by the riptide. I feel light, my thoughts chased away by the waves, my brain washed clean by wind. I want the ocean to carry me away, to pull me from myself and birth me like the tide.

Tamils believe that fate is written on top of our heads, immutable, our future stories scratched into our scalps with permanent ink, birth to death. We can't run from it, we can't fight it, we simply accept it—this notion that we're doomed to pay for the sins we committed in our past lives.

Before I got married, Amma brought Kris's horoscope and mine to an astrologer who told her we were a seventy-five percent match, and that all the indicators pointed to our having had a connection in a past life. Amma was thrilled. A match made in heaven, or rather, written on top of our heads as our souls traveled through the cosmos from one life to another.

I met Kris in college. He was a lanky boy from India with thick-framed glasses and ruddy skin he hated for its darkness. I met him in a gay and lesbian literature class, and for the longest time I knew him as the other South Asian queer on campus. He was pompous, and drove me crazy with the way he turned up his nose at books that weren't part of the British canon, how he refused to look waiters in the eye. We would meet at parties, fight about the meaning of the Vedas or the true class issues in the Kama Sutra, but we didn't become friends until his parents disowned him for being gay. He sought me out at a party, pulled me aside, and said, "I told my mother."

"And?"

His chin, thin and sprinkled with sparse black hairs, quivered. "It was so stupid."

His grief bent him toward me. He put his forehead on my shoulder, and just like that we were friends, bonded by our proximity to the cliff, our danger of falling.

⁓

Our friendship passed in a blur of booze and parties. Kris and I knew enough people that we never had to get involved in the drama of any one social group. We rode to parties with Juan, the boy Kris dated on and off and the only person we knew with a car. Kris sat in the backseat with me, parting my hair in different ways and fussing with my shirt.

Sometimes I met girls at parties but usually I met men. None of them saw me. I wanted it that way.

At one party, Juan danced with a girl while Kris danced by himself near the edge of the crowd.

"Coldhearted," said one of the guys next to me. He was blond and tall and spoke to no one in particular.

"Who?"

"My girlfriend." He raised his bottle toward the dance floor. "I'm Derek." He had at least a foot on me height-wise, so that when he looked at me he seemed to be bending down.

"Lucky."

"Who's lucky?"

"That's my name. Lucky."

The girl pressed against Juan, her lips on his.

Derek pointed at the door and followed me out onto the deck. Summer air pressed on my skin. He pulled out a packet of Pall Malls and offered one to me.

"You're hot," he said. He lit the cigarette I held between my teeth.

I breathed the smoke in deep, held it there until it burst out in a cough.

"Where are you from?" he asked.

"Boston."

"No," he laughed. "Like your parents. Where are they from?"

"Sri Lanka."

"You're all butch hot. I like that."

Nisha would've liked him, would've thought he was cute. He talked about his ex-girlfriend, moving closer so that his arm brushed against my waist. He bent down and kissed me in a cloud of sweat and deodorant.

I was too numb to care, too drunk and a fuck was a fuck.

Derek picked me up and carried me inside the house and up the stairs. I hung onto his neck, the Pall Mall still dangling between my fingers. I wanted to walk but I was too drunk to squirm out of his hold.

He took me to a room on the second floor and sat down on a couch, pulling me down on top of him. I wondered if Kris was looking for me. I wondered if I should leave. I stared at the ceiling and the patterns in the popcorn spackle. Derek was hard.

"I should go," I said.

"Stay the night. I live here."

I got up. He grabbed my arm.

"Stay," he said. He pushed me down and unbuttoned my shirt. He left patches of wet saliva on my skin that cooled with the air.

The ceiling was patterned like the stars, a Big Dipper here, an Orion's Belt there.

When he tried to take off my pants I held his wrist. He lay down on top of me and ground his hips into mine. I tried to focus on the ceiling but I couldn't. He started to grunt.

I wiggled out from under him. "I have to go." I picked up my bra from the floor and put it on.

Derek watched me and lit a cigarette. "My ex, she was butch hot too."

I buttoned up my shirt.

He kept watching. "Now she calls herself a lesbian."

I didn't know if I was supposed to apologize. I said nothing and left, closing the door on the smoke.

In the winter of my senior year, Amma stopped talking to me when she found old texts from an ex-girlfriend, texts like *I miss you* and *I want to fuck you deep and lick my fingers clean* and *Come back to me let's try to make it work.* She had snooped through my phone when I was sleeping. I don't know what tipped her off, what gave her the feeling that something was wrong, but one night when I was home for Christmas break, I awoke to her crying. She clutched my phone to her chest and sobbed at the end of my bed.

I went to a friend's house that night, and stayed there until my bus back to college. Amma stopped transferring money to my account. I wasn't talking to Appa at the time, too angry about the divorce and his remarriage. Vidya was busy with work, Shyama with her husband and grad school, and I wasn't out to either of them. I had $243 to my name.

I put up a website with my art but I was new on the scene and no one wanted to buy it. I sold off my possessions one by one: small green desk, forty dollars; pleather office chair, fifty dollars; blue couch, best offer. The due date for my rent came and went. I sold my furniture, my band posters, the iPod Appa had given me for my birthday. I packed up extra clothes and took them to a consignment store for forty-seven dollars in cash. No job openings. No skills. A rapidly depleting bank account. Kris was luckier—his parents had paid for an entire year of his room and board in the dorms before he came out to them. He snuck out food from the cafeterias for me to eat. Every day he came by my efficiency apartment and we talked ourselves in circles.

"Maybe the loans will come through," I said. I knew that wasn't possible, but I said it anyway. The credit union told us we needed a cosigner.

Kris stacked and unstacked my shot glasses to pass the time. "I wish we could afford to get drunk."

My landlady knocked on the door. Her ragged outline showed through the blinds, the flowered robe she always wore. When I opened the door she was wringing her hands.

Her watery eyes darted to where Kris sat on the floor, roamed over the emptiness of the apartment. "I need your rent, dear. It was due three weeks ago."

"I'll have it soon."

She took a step toward the apartment like she was going to come in. Rightfully I couldn't stop her.

"I need that rent."

"I know. I just don't have it right now."

She looked where the couch used to be. "You going somewhere, dear?"

"No, just—just redecorating."

She frowned and retied the knot around her waist. "Can you make the rent?"

"I just need more time."

"I don't have time, dear. I got someone who wants to rent, and all my rooms are full." She looked at Kris. "He your boyfriend?"

"No."

"I don't like men staying the night."

"He's just a friend."

She poked her finger into the knot of her robe and pulled it back out. "I think I'm going to ask you to move out. I've gotten complaints from the neighbors. Too much noise, too many people over."

"I'll get the rent to you soon, I promise."

"No, no. I want you out. You got two weeks, dear."

I slammed the door closed behind her. I didn't realize I was shaking until Kris pulled me down to the floor between his legs and put his arms around me.

"You can live with me," he said.

"What about your roommate?"

"I'll ask him. Don't worry about it."

⁓

Kris's roommate was a boy named Tim who always wore a Wildcats ball cap and had a Nickelback poster taped to the wall on his side of the room. I slept on his futon, but I had to wait until he was done studying on it every night. It got harder and harder to wake up for my eight-thirty Matrix Theory class. I started skipping it.

On most days, even though the weather was still cold and there was a March bite to the air, I spent my days under the trees on campus, listening to the squirrels coming out for the spring. The trees budded in silk curtains hanging down into the grass. I avoided the room as much as possible. As the weeks dragged on, Tim became more and more talkative.

"You and Kris dating?" he asked me.

"No."

He rubbed the back of his neck and shuffled his feet. "Do you want to go to a movie sometime?"

"I can't."

"I'm a nice guy."

"I'm gay."

He turned back to his Calculus and stayed quiet for a while. I kept writing my English paper.

"You ever slept with a guy?" he asked.

"No."

"Then how do you know?" He kept reading his math book,

following the words with his finger. "I think you just decided too fast."

One weekend Tim had his friends over to the room to drink. They made Jell-O shots in the small microwave and mini fridge. I couldn't afford the booze so Kris and I spent the evening on the dirty, pilled couches in the lounge, playing cards and drinking hot chocolate he'd snuck out from the cafeteria.

Kris shuffled cards without looking at them. "Semester's almost over. What are we going to do?"

"We could go back to Boston after graduation."

Kris stopped shuffling.

"Maybe we can get jobs."

"Maybe you can. No visa, no job for me."

He dealt out the cards into two piles. I picked one up from my pile and turned it over. Jack of Clubs. I ran my finger along the edge of it, letting its sharpness bite into my flesh.

He tapped his fingers on the table. "We could get married."

I dropped the card.

He wasn't smiling. "Think about it. You need to convince your parents you're straight. I need to stay in this country. Your parents would welcome you back."

The room needed more air. I wanted to feel the cold spring night around me. The idea was too sticky. Too many things to go wrong.

"People do it all the time back home," he said.

A marriage of convenience. Amma would talk to me again.

I straightened my pile of cards and gave it to Kris. "Let's go back to the room. I'm tired."

We walked in silence. The dorm floor was especially loud. Students rode scooters back and forth in the hallway. Music clashed through open doorways.

Kris's room was dark. Someone had thrown towels over the lamps so that they glowed eerie and muted. At least ten people sat crammed onto the floor and the futon.

Tim got up and stumbled toward us. He put the tips of his fingers together around the red cup he was holding. He bowed. "Namaste."

I grabbed Kris's arm and pulled him back toward the door.

"What?" Tim stood up straight. "Isn't that how you guys do it?"

I opened the door. He crossed the room and closed it. He put his elbow on the door near my head. I could smell his sweat.

"You're Indian and gay." He turned toward the room of people. Some laughed. "How does that work out?"

"It works just fine," I said.

He lurched forward and kissed me. My head slammed against the door. My brain rang.

Kris wrenched him backward but he pushed his way toward me. I pressed against the door.

He was too close. "I think you're lying."

No escape. I pushed back, pushed hard, away. He fell. Laughter from the walls. Red cup spilled red fizz into the carpet. He pushed me down into a beanbag. I stood up. Pushed down. Up, pushed down, my knees gave way again and again not strong enough to stand up push back, push hard, away away away again push push run.

I ran to the pond and collapsed into the trunk of a tree. I watched the water. I wanted something to wilt against. Kris found me. He was carrying my jacket. He held it out to me and I put it on. The fabric was freezing. He'd been looking for a while.

He sat next to me and stared across the water. Clumps of ice had started to form on the pond, little veins spreading across the top like spiderwebs, eating up the warmth.

"I love you," he said. "I hope you know that."

I watched a duck jump into the water. The ice—too fragile still—cracked and broke. Water rippled from beneath the bird's feathers and spread out across the pond.

My breath curled white and smoky out of me. "If we do this—if we get married, what happens when we fall in love?"

"Tell you what. If Nisha ever decides she wants to marry you, I'll give you a divorce."

"Nisha and I haven't talked in four years," I said.

Kris laughed. "Then you don't have to worry about that particular scenario."

I watched the bird on the pond, the ice breaking. We could still win.

After we get back from the beach, Nisha stops answering my calls. During the day, she texts me that she needs space away from me to get her head around this marriage. At night, she wants me to say "I love you" and describe in detail how I'd fuck her. When I ask to meet up, she refuses. I turn off my phone and stop answering her texts.

Grandmother sits outside every weekday for hours at a time, bundled in more and more clothing as the temperature drops. She doesn't risk it when Amma's at home during the weekends. And even though she never comes out and asks me, I know I'm supposed to keep quiet about what she does all day.

By the end of October, the temperature is too cold to sit

outside for more than an hour. I try to coax Grandmother back inside, and some days she surrenders. Some days the smell of betel leaves and the sound of her favorite shows are enough. But other days she cups her hand behind her ear and tells me to listen to the baby.

"It's your baby, Vidya."

"I'm Lucky."

"It's your baby."

So I bring her more blankets, start making her wear her winter coat. She comes inside right before Amma gets home. Her skin is icy to the touch, the wrinkles still holding pockets of cold between the tissue.

One day it rains. When I come downstairs to drink my coffee, Grandmother is sitting outside without her winter coat. Everything is soaked. Rain blurs her face.

I run outside.

"Come in the house," I say.

Thunder grumbles overhead. The rain is cold, little pinpricks to my skin. It rattles on the tin gutters. Rain pelts Grandmother's skin. She shivers. Her cotton housecoat clings to her legs.

I shake her arm. "Come on, Ammamma." I squint to see through the rain, and try again in the best Tamil I can muster. "Vaango, vaango."

She gets up slowly. Each step takes a thousand raindrops. I pull her inside and slam the door shut. The rain has soaked into the carpet inside.

I run and grab towels from the bathroom and when I get back she's still standing where I left her, soaked and shivering. I throw a towel on her head and mop up as much of the water as I can.

"You need to change," I say.

Her eyes look through me.

"Neenga uduppa maathonum," I try again, in Tamil.

She moves toward the bathroom. I get a sweater and thick socks from her room and bring them down. When she takes too long to change, I pound my knuckles on the bathroom door. She comes out dry, her eyes clear. I wrap a blanket around her over the sweater.

"You need to change your clothes, Vidya," she says. "You'll get sick."

I put on dry clothes and clean up most of the water from the carpet. Grandmother sits in the kitchen while I make tea. My hands won't stay steady. I watch to make sure she drinks it all. My tea tastes like rain on metal and musty carpet. I already know I won't tell Amma about this.

⁓

After Nisha's engagement, Amma cries often about wanting me to have a baby, to fit in for once in my life and be a good brown daughter. She cries when I'm helping her cook, when we drink tea, before she goes to sleep. I hear her wheezing, see the way she trembles with the effort.

One day she stays home from work and claims her heart is hurting.

"I think it's a heart attack," she says. She's burrowed in her blankets, only her head visible in the enormous folds of her comforter.

"Your heart is fine," I say.

"It feels like stabbing. My daughter is giving me a heart attack." She rubs at her chest and cries.

I sit there, trying to feel my own pulse, my blood, some primordial pull to comfort my mother, a tear, something, anything to reassure me that I'm still alive. Instead all I feel is numbness reaching to the tips of my fingers, something cold and hard in me pushing back against her tears.

"I miss Kris," I tell her. "I think I should go and visit him."

What I really miss is the way Nisha's skin smells and how she smiles when I kiss her. She still won't answer my calls. She still refuses to meet up.

I summon up every last dreg of compassion I have left. I rub Amma's chest for her and get her some aspirin. Maybe that softness does it, because she smiles for the first time in days. "Go home and spend some time with your husband," she says.

Kris isn't home when my Camry finally pulls into our driveway. I'm exhausted and dizzy at the sight of our lavender front door and black shutters. I drag my duffel bag into the house, get myself a beer, and sink into our couch to look out the window at the street. The living room is just as I left it—messy, Kris's computer thrown onto a couch seat, weeks-old bowls of ramen in muddy water, fat fruit flies meandering through the air, the sharp, sweet smell of rotting garbage. After the immaculate cleanliness of Amma's house, our living room makes me queasy.

I drink my beer and watch the cars that march by our house. The numbness sits inside me, makes time slip by while I stand still.

When Kris comes home I'm still sitting there, looking out the window and watching the sunset. Not even the colors can get inside my skin.

He flips on the light switch. "How many beers have you had?" He toes off his black leather loafers and loosens his tie.

I point at the couch armrest where I've stacked my beer caps into a tower. Who's counting? The slush in my brain feels good after Amma's house, the sluggishness against that stonehearted feeling, the engagement, Nisha, Tasha, Amma, all of them pulling me in different directions.

"Jesus." Kris counts out the beer caps one by one. "Nine." He takes them into the kitchen, and comes back with a glass of gin and tonic. He unbuttons his collar and takes off his belt. "So are we getting drunk or what?"

"I suppose. Everything's fucked up." I can feel the steam leaving me, my legs itching to get up and move.

He sits across from me and drinks.

"Amma wants us to have a baby. Can you believe that? Us, with a baby. God."

"What's wrong with that?"

I put my beer bottle on the coffee table. The mud in my mind wobbles. "Are you serious? You know what's wrong with that." The walls look squishy. I could pinch them with my fingers.

He stares at his glass, collecting the condensation on its side with a finger. "I think a baby sounds nice." He flicks droplets of water at me.

"As long as you carry it."

"Come on, Lucky. A baby would be good for us. Think about it. We'd be a real family." He reaches over and pushes a piece of hair off my forehead.

"Don't touch me."

He wants to take back the moment he came out to his mother, take back her locking him in his room, take back his imprisonment in his parents' house for days before he snuck out and took a cab to the airport so he could fly back to the States.

"We're fucked up." The words warp around my tongue. "We've fucked this up. We can't fuck up someone else."

"We could make really good parents. Think about it." He drains the last of his gin and tonic and vanishes up the stairs, glass in hand.

I want him to come back, to smile and laugh like we used to in college, in the first months of our marriage, that delight at having pulled the wool over everyone's eyes.

⌒

Kris shakes me awake. I'm still on the couch, still in my clothes, my duffel bag still sitting on the floor of the living room.

I sit up. Sunshine clangs behind my eyes. "Don't let me do that again. I'm too damn old."

He gives me a glass of water and I drain it.

"So." He sits across from me in the same armchair as the night before. "About this baby."

"The baby we're not going to have? Yes, what about it?"

He rubs his forehead and stands up. He goes to the kitchen with my empty glass.

I shut my eyes, hoping my head will stop throbbing.

He comes back with a full glass and an envelope. Dirt encrusts its corners. "This came for you. I think it's from Vidya."

He lays the envelope down on the coffee table. A part of me doesn't want to look at it. A ghost. An empty chair. I pick it up and there it is, her writing, the spikey *t*'s and long *p*'s that dig into the depths of the next line, addressed to an apartment we haven't lived in for two years. Postmarked a week ago. I take it in my hand. I carefully run my finger underneath the flap, which comes away easily, the glue weakened with travel. Inside, a short letter written on thick white paper that's embedded with what looks like seeds. The letter is wrapped around a glossy photo. Vidya stands next to a palm tree, squinting at the sun, dressed in a skirt and a T-shirt. On her hip, a little girl of maybe three, her hair curling in and out, wrestled into pigtails. The girl is darker than Vidya, her mouth thicker, her nose wider. She holds onto Vidya with one chubby hand, and reaches out to the camera with the other.

Lucky, I'm sorry I missed your wedding all those years ago. You know I had my reservations, but I'm happy for you. I hope he's everything you wanted in a husband. I miss you. I'm doing great. Radha, my daughter, makes my life so happy. You, Grandmother and Amma are in my thoughts. Give my love. Vidya. P.S. You can plant the letter. It'll grow wildflowers.

I flip the letter. Nothing on the other side.

Kris holds out the envelope. "There's a return address. Kentucky."

For the next few days I'm on the Internet, trying to track down the address, match it with a phone number or email. I try Vidya's old email address. She hasn't answered any email I've sent in the last five years. No luck on a phone number. I check everything I can find, including preschools and kindergartens in the area to see if a little girl named Radha goes there. They turn me away. Confidentiality issues. I call Shyama but she hasn't heard from Vidya, either. Even Vidya's art site, the online portfolio where she used to post pictures of her sculptures, is gone, just as it had been right after she ran away.

I find nothing. She has made sure to leave emptiness behind.

My sister Vidya left at night. She didn't tell anyone she was going, but I remember her coming into my room right as I was falling asleep. I had just graduated college, and we were all busy planning my wedding to Kris.

The corner of my bed sagged. She put her fingers through my then-long hair, again and again, until I melted back into sleep, lulled by the rhythm of her nails on my scalp.

The day before she left, she and Amma got into a fight. They fought often, about everything from what Vidya wore—Amma said it was too revealing—to what she did in her free time—Amma had wanted her to volunteer at the hospital to help her get into med school, but Vidya wanted to teach an art class at the county jail. This fight was different. Amma had found a Valentine's Day card addressed to Vidya from someone named Jamal.

Vidya and Amma faced each other in the kitchen. I hid myself behind the curve of the staircase and watched.

Amma waved the pink, glittery card above her head. "You're not American. You're not like these American girls. You can't run around with boys at your age." She crumpled the card in her fist and shook it. "What will people think?"

Vidya clenched her fingers at her sides. "I love Jamal." She was wearing the cutoff shorts that Amma hated.

I sat down on the stairs and pushed my toes into the thick carpet.

"It won't last, Vidya." Amma's voice softened and she sank into a chair. "Love covers up all the bad things, but then when it's gone, the bad things will still be there."

Vidya put her hands on Amma's head. "Nothing bad will happen."

"People like him don't know the meaning of a good marriage."

Vidya snatched her hands away like Amma had burned her. "People like him?"

"An Indian man will love you forever."

"Like Appa did?"

Appa and Amma had told us they were splitting up on the day of Vidya's graduation from college. The news was slipped in between congratulations and anxiety about medical school. Appa moved out of our house at the same time that Vidya moved back in to start a new job as a pharmaceutical lab tech for the summer. By fall, Appa had married Laila Aunty and bought a house in the rich part of Lexington.

The day after the fight, Vidya disappeared, no note. We woke up in the morning and she was gone. She had taken most of her clothes—billowy chiffon blouses and designer jeans with studded back pockets. The only things left in her suddenly empty closet were the churidars and sarees that Amma had bought for her, now lonely on their plastic hangers.

Amma sat in Vidya's room for hours, spreading them out on the bed, running her fingers over and over them, tracing the patterns of flowers and peacocks embroidered on silk.

⁓

"Maybe I should just go down to Kentucky." I stand at the door to Kris's bedroom. He lies on the bed in graying boxer briefs, partly covered by a fuzzy quilt. Thick curtains block out the morning sun. I walk the rest of the way into the room and lay down next to him.

"A baby boy is a joy to have. I should write that one down." He taps his chin with a long finger. "How about, 'The stork is on his way'?"

I try to punch him but he rolls away.

"Or 'I hope you've caught up on sleep. Congrats.'"

"You're an ass." His room is filthy—clothes everywhere, shoes kicked off near the bed, two towels draped over the tufted leather headboard. "Was Justin staying over while I was gone?"

"I think you should go to Kentucky. I think you should find her, and bring her back."

"Really?"

"No. If she wanted to be found, she would've said so. She would've given you a phone number, email address, something."

"There was a return address."

"Who knows if it's real?"

I remember the empty whiteness of the letter. The note, really, the jagged letters contained in a rectangle in the middle

156

of the page, surrounded by nothing. I could go pull it out from under my pillow where I stuffed it the night before, run my skin over the paper, see if I missed something.

"'Life isn't fair,'" Kris says. "'Get well soon.' No, that's shitty. And yes, Justin was staying over."

"Where is he?"

"He left for California a week ago."

"Are you okay with that?" I ask.

He flips over onto his back so we're lying side by side. He stares up at the ceiling, and says with that high, fake voice he uses when he lies, "Of course I'm okay. I'm always okay."

Kris proposes a night out. He wants to leave at eight, which really means nine, because as per usual we don't start getting ready until seven forty-five. I hated his chronic lateness for years, but I got used to it because I knew that if I didn't, I would turn into Appa, pacing anxiously in the living room while Amma got ready and then fighting the whole way in the car. Too many fights.

Kris tries on outfits while I watch. I spread out on his bed in my boxers and feel the air on my skin for the first time in months.

"Are these pants too tight?" He turns around in front of his mirror to scrutinize his butt.

"Criminally."

He takes a bow. "These are perfect. You should get ready, too."

"I like being naked." Amma has rules about clothing. Pajamas can't be worn during the day. You can't leave the house in jeans and T-shirts. Hair has to be combed. No cleavage. No shorts or skirts above the knee. Sports bras only when exercising. No men's clothes.

"Get dressed," Kris says.

"Pick something out for me."

"How butch?"

"Futch."

He disappears down the hallway and into my room. "Can you fit into those red jeans I bought you?"

"Too tight."

"They're supposed to be tight."

"I'm a little fat right now."

He comes back with jeans draped over his arm, holding a stack of shirts on hangers. He stops in the doorway. "You aren't fat right now."

He wrestles me into a short sleeved button-down shirt and tie and fusses with my hair.

The phone rings. Amma, with news that Grandmother is in the hospital again—this time with pneumonia. We leave immediately for Boston.

Cars skid along the highway, their tires fogged by rain-slicked tar, their metal scuttling under rusty green bridges. The robotic voice of the GPS guides me. Even though I know the way, I always turn on the GPS like Amma taught me to. Her voice still lives in my head.

The rain. It was the rain. Grandmother got sick because of the rain.

When I park in the hospital lot, Kris reaches over and takes off my tie. He undoes the top button of my shirt and untucks the back. "Well, this is as feminine as it's going to get. Just act extra girly."

The smell of antiseptic and sickness crawls under my skin. Death is everywhere in a hospital, as common and concentrated as the disinfected air. Grandmother floats among the tubes and machines, scratchy white sheets draped around her like a coat, the small room crammed with steady beeping.

I sit on the couch while Grandmother sleeps. Kris escapes to go buy coffee with Appa. Amma cries silently near a small window that faces the night's darkness.

Grandmother lies motionless except for her raspy breathing and spasming eyelids. Her mouth hangs open.

Amma stares blankly out the window. "I should've brought her in earlier. She's been coughing for a while." She shudders, her voice almost muffled out by the beeping of machines.

"You couldn't have seen this coming," I say.

Amma looks me up and down. "Why are you dressed like a boy?" She doesn't wait for me to answer, just turns back to the window.

Grandmother doesn't have her dentures in and her mouth looks sunken like a cave. I sit and watch her while the scent of the hospital works its way into my clothes. Grandmother caught me with Nisha once when we were in middle school. Nisha and I had hidden in my room to play out a scene we'd read in a summer reading book for school. A ronin warrior slowly strips off his mistress's kimono, revealing her part by part, each second written in detail. Grandmother's face had hardened when she found us, her voice glass-like when she asked us what the hell we were doing.

I stare at Grandmother's sleeping form because when I look away all I can see is the rain soaking into her dress, her face and hair dripping with it, her thin body shivering, rain pooling into the carpet, her eyes that day—the clarity as if the rain had washed away her dementia and for a moment she had herself back.

"It's from sitting out in the cold," Amma says. "Why did you let her sit out there in the cold?"

"It's no one's fault."

"I told you not to let her."

I stroke Grandmother's hand. Her skin moves in many folds.

"She's had a hard life." Amma's voice is softer now, sadder, choked up. "What will I do if she doesn't—What will I do?"

Something gives. The hardness inside me budges, just for a moment. I walk over to Amma and put my hand on her shoulder.

~

Grandmother doesn't wake up until morning. Kris sleeps on one of the chairs with his head drooping to the side. Amma and Appa sit silently on the couch. I sit on Grandmother's bed, rubbing her hand and nodding off every once in a while with my head in my hand.

Around sunrise, Grandmother's hand twitches in mine. I snap my head up, but my eyes are heavy.

"Ammamma?"

Her eyes open and scan the ceiling. She looks through me, her eyes cloudy.

"Vidya." Her lips quiver into a smile.

I nod. Amma comes and puts her hand on Grandmother's forehead.

"I want to see Vidya's baby." Grandmother struggles to shake the words from her mouth. "I want to see Vidya's baby."

Amma is going to cry again. Appa comes to her side and rubs his hand up and down her arm.

Kris and I drive home after Grandmother is released from the hospital and settled back home with Amma. Hollowness eats its way through me, my insides scooped out and left on the floor of Grandmother's hospital room. Kris stays silent in the passenger seat and squints through the windshield without blinking. The sky hangs a uniform gray against the gold dead grass in the median. Rain rises like mist through the spindly trees that flank the highway. The car shifts beneath me, slides along, bouncing back and forth between the white dotted lines.

I'm skin stretched around bones, my chest cavernous, no heart, my head dizzy with its own emptiness. The sun sets and still the road winds, pitch black except for the lone headlights of my car. When we first moved away from the city, I was terrified of driving at night, of plunging through the thick blackness, hoping I would see the next turn in time. But now it's easy, like walking through our house in the dark, using my fingers and the pressure around me to know the way.

I turn off the car in our driveway, unlock the house with my hollow fingers, walk up to my bedroom, and lie facedown on my bed. I don't want to move for days. Grandmother wants to see Vidya, and her baby.

Kris sits down on the edge of the bed. "She's going to be okay."

I try to breathe out the concrete that's filling me up.

"I'm sick of you being sick," Kris says, so quietly that I can barely hear him. "Get well soon."

I sit up and with all my strength, I push him down onto the bed and pin his arms above his head. I want to punch him, see the trickle of blood from his nose, feel my fist on his cheek. His skin would give way and then his muscles, ripping through, crack and shatter. I wrap one hand around his throat. I push my thumb and index finger into his arteries. He swallows. I push harder. His breathing slows. Grandmother wants to see Vidya. Vidya, the photo of her and her daughter, the little girl's hands reaching for the camera. Grandmother's housecoat soaked with rain, her wheezing cough, her hospital blankets and the drip drip drip of saline. Would it be so bad? I like the softness of baby skin, the way their limbs squish and smell like milk. Kris and I would be good enough parents.

"Let's have a baby," I say.

Kris stares at me. I loosen the pressure on his neck. He coughs once, twice. "Let's."

I've pushed the sound out of him. I bend down and kiss him. We've kissed before, when we were drunk and it seemed like a funny thing to do. We know how to kiss each other. We fumble off our clothes. We know the moves. We're skilled enough to make it work. I press my face into the pillow and try to pretend it's not Kris fucking me. I'm too full too full, dirty with the movement, Kris grabbing my hip to make me stop and it drips down my legs I want it out of me out out bled dry. I run to the bathroom and throw myself into the shower.

I move back to Amma's house to take care of Grandmother. Constant supervision, doctor's orders. She sleeps most mornings. Around eleven I help her come down the stairs, holding her by the arm. I make her tea, help her to the folding chair, and watch Tamil game shows with her while I catch up on commission deadlines. I help her use the bathroom, get her water and juice when she asks.

After a few days, boredom settles inside me and makes my limbs twitch with the urge to move—dance, play rugby, anything. I think about calling Nisha, but my stomach knots with nausea when I pick up the phone. I want to visit the rugby house, but I don't want to explain the rain, explain Grandmother. So instead I call the Mason Jar, and find out they have an open stage night where anyone can dance.

I park outside the Mason Jar and wait. I'm early. The place is still dark inside the windows, though there are a couple of businessmen at the bar. My hands tremble on the steering wheel. I can't make myself go in. I watch the door. For a long time it stays closed, but then a woman in a long skirt opens it and walks in. I've brought a couple of dancing outfits I wore for performances in college—not Bharatanatyam but Bollywood songs. I still remember the choreography from some of them. I can do this. I'm a dancer. I trained for years. I can do this.

I cross the street to the bar and open the door. A bouncer sits on a stool. The place is darkened with thick drapes hung over the windows. Over-varnished wood tables, black leather booths, gothic chandeliers, black-and-white tile floors, a scuffed wooden stage on the far end of the room.

"I'm here for the open stage." I grip my bag of costumes tight.

The bouncer motions to the bar. "Mr. Alan, got another one for you."

A man in a green trench coat turns on his wooden barstool. He's mostly bald but a few wisps of white hair still cling onto the skin above his ears. He has tiny, watery eyes. He takes the toothpick out of his martini and sucks off one brown olive.

"You from India?" He picks off the other olive with his hand and pops it in his mouth, licking his fingers clean.

I walk to the bar so I don't have to shout.

"You know how to belly dance?" he asks. "We need a belly dancer."

"I thought it was open stage."

He picks his teeth with the toothpick. "I like to get a handle on what everyone's going to perform."

"A Bollywood song."

He hops down from the chair, landing a full head shorter than me. "What's your name, sweetheart?"

"Lucky."

"I'm sorry, what?"

"Lucky."

"That won't do. Won't do at all." He turns toward the back of the bar and gestures for me to follow. "Jasmine? No, too common."

We walk through a set of curtains behind the stage into a hallway.

"Asha? Yes, Asha. Asha okay with you? I have a cousin who married an Asha."

"My name's Lucky."

He points at me. "Tonight, your name's Asha." He opens a door to a room. "This is where the girls get dressed."

The tiny room has a couch squeezed into one corner and full-length mirrors nailed to the wall. Three women scuttle around in various stages of undress.

Mr. Alan claps his hands and the girls turn around. "Ladies, ladies. I want you to meet Asha. She's doing Bollywood tonight."

He walks back through the set of curtains to the bar. I push the door open a little more and go into the dressing room. One girl with milky skin and a thin face smiles at me. Her lips are painted dark brown and her light blue eyes lined heavily with black. She wears a long quilted skirt and a fringed scarf.

She holds out her hand. "I'm Mala. You're going to love it."

I shake her hand. The others introduce themselves. They all have these brown-sounding stage names, but none of them are brown. I dress in a mirrored lehenga choli and drape the dupatta around me like a saree. The girls ooh and aah over the embroidery and the bangles.

Mala picks up a sheet of bindis. "Can I borrow one of these?" She plucks one off and sticks it in the middle of her forehead. She plucks another and sticks it on my forehead.

I take it off and move it down to between my eyebrows.

"You got any perfume?" Mala asks.

"No."

She digs in one of her bags and pulls out a vial. "We always wear perfume. The men like it." She spritzes some on me.

My eyes water. I smell like a baby hooker.

Mr. Alan brings back shots of tequila. A couple more girls join us. Most of them are doing some type of belly dance, going by the outfits. We wait in the room while the murmur of the bar gets louder. By nine thirty, there's a steady hum of conversation. Mr. Alan comes back to decide the order of performance.

"I need to leave early," I say.

He mimes shooting a gun at me. "Then you're first, Asha."

I take two more shots of tequila and follow him out to the bar area. He climbs up onstage. "This here's our newest girl, Asha."

I walk up onstage. Some of the men in the front hoot and shout. The place is packed and dim. I make eye contact with the back wall. That's how Nisha taught me to overcome my stage fright when we were young. "Watch the back wall, and never look away. Everyone will think you're looking at them."

The music starts, and it's easier to tune out the shouts from the men. First muted drumbeats, thaam thaam theem, thaam thaam theem, then flute arching over, low sitar plucks, a rumbling cello. I breathe steady and clear my head. It's just another performance. I've done this hundreds of times. Arm waves, hip circles, spin. Nothing else exists but me and the wood under my feet. I remember the music. Thaam thaam theem. Thaam thaam theem. Step out, back, out, back, hands left and right, wrists flowing like waves.

⁓

It isn't until I'm back in the dressing room that I hear the clapping and shouting in the bar. Mr. Alan comes in. "Hear that? They like you." He holds out another tequila shot. "A couple of guys requested private dances with you. Your choice, of course."

I stand up too fast and the room lurches. I hold the edge of the couch.

He comes toward me like he's going to help. My stomach spasms. If he touches me I'll puke. I grab hold of my costume bag, and push my way past him. A couple of men call out to me as I push my way through the bar.

Tasha invites me to the rugby house. I miss its exposed beams, the cracks running along the plaster walls, Jesse with her tough posturing. I pick Tasha up after work at a bank downtown.

She throws herself into the front seat. "What are you so happy about?" But she's grinning, too.

"Where to?"

Her smile slips off. She takes a long time with her seat belt. "I know I invited you to the rugby house. But Jesse—well, we didn't know how to say no so—well, Nisha's over there. Right now."

I don't know how much they know. I put the car in drive and head toward JP.

"I don't care if Nisha's there. We're all adults, I'm sure we can be civilized."

When we pull up the hill, Jesse and Nisha are outside on the deck with a few others, sitting on the mismatched chairs and on the railing. Nisha laughs with her hand on Jesse's arm. I push my hands into my jean pockets and try not to scowl.

Tasha starts to climb the steep hill toward the house. "You sure you're going to be okay?"

"I'll be fine."

"I should warn you. Nisha thinks that we're—you and I—you know, that we're together."

I stop walking. "Where did she get that idea?"

Tasha kicks at a dark stain on the sidewalk. "Something I said, I think. I could've corrected her. But I didn't. I let her believe it."

"I don't care what Nisha thinks."

We walk up to the house in step. We're close enough that the hairs on our arms mingle. Nisha doesn't look at us, engrossed in a conversation with a girl I don't know. Is everyone quieter now that we're here? Our steps creak too loud on the porch. Tasha stands closer than she should.

Jesse crosses the deck, wraps her enormous arms around me, and claps me on the back. She raises her cigarette as if in toast and puts it in between her thin lips. The tip glows as she sucks in. She slings an arm over my shoulder.

I try not to look at Nisha, who stands directly opposite me, still with her head turned away. She talks to a girl I don't know, every once in a while touching her dangling earrings like she's afraid they've fallen off. The girl she's talking to is feminine and Asian, pretty with long dark hair that falls around her face. I try not to stare at Nisha, try to focus on my conversation with Jesse. My eyes wander back and forth.

"You should've seen this talent show," Jesse says. "We wrote the lyrics on our stomachs and spelled out the song."

Tasha talks to another girl I don't know—a mohawked red-head with snakebite lip piercings. She hangs on Tasha's arm and looks at her with a dimpled smile.

"Harder, faster, stronger," Jesse says. "You know the song, right?"

Nisha has her blue contacts in. I like her eyes brown, but I could never talk her out of wearing them.

When the already dark sky starts to spit down rain, the other girls leave. The mohawked girl kisses Tasha goodbye. Nisha stays behind and talks to Jesse.

Tasha comes over. Our arms brush but she doesn't flinch away. She leans close to my ear and whispers, "I guess that wasn't very convincing." She smells like old cologne.

If I turn, we'd be too close. "Whatever she wants to believe."

Nisha's cold, glassy eyes look at me. It takes forever for her to cross the deck. I see her mouth make the words before I hear them.

"I need to talk to you." She turns around and heads into the house.

Tasha puts a hand on my shoulder. "You don't have to go."

I follow Nisha into the house. She sits down on the bed in the living room—Tasha's bed. She pats the space next to her and crosses her legs, arranging her crocheted skirt so that it reveals just one tanned kneecap. I stand near the door. She pats the bed again.

The TV plays on mute, an old movie about a Jewish lesbian in Berlin during the Holocaust, trying to fly under the radar. Unseen, hunted, dangerous.

I sit on the low couch that faces the bed. From this seat I have to look up at Nisha, framed by Tasha's paintings on the wall.

The Jewish woman in the movie is vacationing with her lover and her lover's children, taking pictures in wooded areas.

"I've been thinking." Nisha frowns and rubs down her skirt. "I know we don't have bridal parties, but if my wedding was a white wedding, you'd be my maid of honor."

The woman on TV is found out—Nazi officers drag her down the stairs of her German lover's apartment building. Dirt stains her white pantsuit.

"It's stupid to be fighting with my maid of honor."

I can't feel my skin, only the heaviness and my stomach turning. I wish I'd never left Amma's house. Behind Nisha's head hang three square canvases. I first thought they were close-ups of tree trunks but now I see eyes staring back from the weaving colors.

"Are you listening, Lucky? I said I don't want to fight any-more."

I can't find words. I nod. The Jewish woman's German lover, now old, walks in a garden. She survived the war. Married with children. Hidden. Safe.

"Are we okay then?" Nisha says. "We can go back to normal?"

I stare at the canvases behind her head. The eyes in the wood grain stare back. I can't feel my skin. Normal, where Nisha is engaged and we pretend like she's not, like she's not walking into a new life that has no space for me, where we are both in love and married, just not to each other, normal where us is an impossibility. Hidden, safe. "Yeah, sure. We can go back to normal."

"You stayed out all day." Amma puts her hands on her hips. Several pots and pans hiss behind her on the stove. Her laptop sits open on the dining table next to a stack of dentistry journals. "What use is you staying with me to help if you go out with your friends all day?"

I take my time hanging up my coat in the front closet. "Where's Grandmother?"

"Sleeping." Amma turns her back to me and walks over to the stove. She stirs the contents of each pot. "I must have done something terrible in my past life."

She did something terrible in her past life, and is cursed with daughters who don't listen to her. One who runs away, another who never acts like a brown lady should act. Be a proper woman. Have a child. Where is your natural urge to nurture? Where did it go? Stop being a deviant. Do you have no shame?

I tune her out and rifle through the dentistry journals on the table. *Dysesthesia of the mandible. The effects of beverages on plaque acidogenicity after a sugary challenge. Is it ethical to raffle off prizes in exchange for referrals?*

Nisha calls me crying. She won't tell me why. "I need more outfits," she says instead. "For the wedding." All those pieces of ritual require outfit changes for the bride. "Will you take me?" Nisha's voice is quiet, like she's afraid I might refuse.

I don't want to upset Amma, but she's only too happy to let me go for this. Spending time with family is only important if the alternative is spending it with friends she doesn't approve of.

I drive Nisha to Chandra's Bridal Boutique in Cambridge.

In the window of the tiny, cottage-like shop, three headless mannequins model three types of bridal wear from three different Indian states. Nisha's eyes are still red, her face swollen from crying in the car, but she makes a brave attempt at nonchalance. A bell tinkles when we open the door. The store is small, cramped, and brightly lit, every wall filled with shelves that glitter in rainbow.

"Do you have a new saree for the wedding?" Nisha asks me.

I nod. Amma probably bought one as soon as she heard.

"It better be nice," she says. "Not too simple, okay?"

If Amma picked it out, it definitely won't be simple.

Nisha goes up to the woman behind the counter. "I'm looking for a churidar for the mehendi ceremony before my wedding." If she was white, she would've flashed the diamond on her ring. Sri Lankan weddings don't even have mehendi ceremonies, but Nisha insisted. When we were kids, she was the one who got new dresses and jewelry for no particular reason. My parents' money was split among three kids.

The woman behind the counter pulls out churidars in crinkly plastic bags. Blue and white with beads, yellow and orange with stones, red and green with embroidery. "These are the newest styles. Just came in this week. Very affordable."

Nisha looks down her nose at the churidars on the counter. She looks like Kris. He gets this way in brown stores, as if the salespeople should be bowing to him inside. I want to hold her by the waist, draw her to me.

"Do you have any unique styles?"

"These are the newest styles." The woman pulls out some more churidars from their plastic cases and spreads them out on top of the others. "This style is in all the Indian movies now."

Nisha touches a gold and white churidar. She takes it to the back room to try it on.

The woman turns to me. "Would you like to buy one?" Her black-lined eyes blink behind round glasses.

Nisha opens the door to the fitting room. The woman turns to the shelves and starts putting some of the churidars back. There doesn't seem to be any rhyme or reason to what goes where, but there has to be some code.

"How does it look?" Nisha asks too loudly. She has that scrunched-up face that can either lead to yelling or to tears.

I put on the best awed-by-your-beauty face I can manage. "Looks great. Turn around."

She does a little twirl. The woman behind the counter glances at me over her shoulder.

"Looks great."

"You already said that."

"Just means it's twice as true."

Nisha goes back to the fitting room. The small store's getting hot. I pull at the neck of my shirt to let some air in.

"If she likes that, she may like these." The woman pulls out more churidars. "These are her size."

"I don't think—"

"We have matching jewelry."

Nisha comes out of the dressing room and looks through the churidars that the woman has just pulled out. She's walking with a sway to her hips again, which is a good sign.

"I'll get this." She points to the one she tried on. "And—" She sniffs loudly.

I put a hand on her shoulder but she shrugs it off. She has her back to me. I can't tell if she's going to cry or not.

"Nisha?"

She hides her face and shoves her purse at me. "Pay for this. I'll be in the car." She runs toward the door.

I feel the numbness start to spread. No. It's Nisha. I'm not numb to her.

I turn to the woman behind the counter. "The gold and white churidar. And some matching bangles."

"We have these mirrored ones. Just got them in." She opens the back of the counter and pulls out a set of shimmering bangles. She dangles them on her finger, filling the store with their clinking.

I touch the bangles lightly. They feel like sand from all the glitter, with mirrors embedded deep in the metal. Nisha is crying outside.

I pay with Nisha's money and hurry to my car. She's crying against the passenger door. I unlock it and she gets inside. I get in the driver's side, stare at the steering wheel, and wait.

She's shrunken in on herself, all curled up toward her knees. "You were flirting with her," she says.

"Who? I wasn't."

"You like her." She cries harder.

I punch the side of the steering wheel, making her jump. "You're getting married in a month. What the fuck does anything matter."

She doesn't have her contacts in, her eyes dark brown now like oil. "You're married."

"Kris and I, we have an arrangement."

Tears cling to her eyelashes. She doesn't say anything.

"Nisha, our marriage isn't real. Kris likes men."

She puts her head in her hands. "I can't do this. This isn't me." Her hair swings around her face. "I only agreed to get married because you were married. Why didn't you tell me before?"

She reaches out and grabs my arm. I draw her to me and hold her while she sobs.

"It'll be okay. You'll be fine."

She grabs hold of my wrist and squeezes hard. She looks up at me and her face is wild—her eyes large and her chin set like she's clenching her teeth together. "Let's go. Run away with me."

"What?"

"We could go somewhere. We could be happy somewhere. You and me."

I push her gently away from me. "You can't be serious."

She pulls my wrist. Her fingers grip like a vice. "We could go anywhere. You and me."

I close my eyes and hold her close. The bride belongs to the man who brings her home. "Okay," I say. "You and me."

The days march toward the wedding. Grandmother starts to feel better. She still can't move around much, but she sits and watches her shows. Sometimes she sits in the kitchen and croaks instructions to Amma while she cooks. When it comes to food, Grandmother is lucid. The onions have to be cut smaller, fried longer, with more oil and spices. "Smaller," Grandmother cries. "Don't take that out yet. Put in more curry powder." Amma grinds her teeth and puts up with it. At Grandmother's instructions, Amma stays in the kitchen most nights and during the weekends.

"You need to spend time with her," Amma tells me. "She needs something to occupy her time."

I dig out two pairs of knitting needles and yarn from the recesses of my old closet, along with a how-to-knit book from the eighties. A blond woman with gigantic teeth and a workout headband smiles on the cover. The pages are crisp with too many spilled beverages.

I give Grandmother the thickest needles I can find. I try to start stitches in bulky, fuzzy blue yarn while she squints at the directions.

She puts a betel leaf packet in her mouth and reads while chewing. "Knitting soothes the troubled spirit. To make a purl stitch, the needle is inserted through the front of the stitch, then must be brought forward and over the yarn."

When I get the stitch down, I show her. I stand behind her and guide her arms and hands like she's a human puppet. When I was little, Grandmother knitted blankets, scarves, sweaters, even dresses and gloves. She bought the warmest wool she could find in Sri Lanka, and sent the finished pieces to us through relatives and friends traveling to the US. I hated wearing the brightly-colored sweaters and dresses. My American classmates made fun of me for looking like a FOB.

Grandmother catches on to the stitch slowly, but her fingers still remember how to hold the yarn with tension. We knit to the beat of her chewing and spitting. Her hands tremble as she knits. Without me behind her, guiding her movements, she quickly forgets the stitch and tangles up the yarn. When I look up, she's trying to pick apart a knot with her shaking fingers. I take the yarn from her as gently as I can and put it aside. She coughs. I stand behind her and give her a fresh ball of yarn, guiding her hands as they cast on stitches.

When Amma comes home and finds us knitting, she says, "This is how it should be. You should be learning to have responsibility, not running around with friends like a little kid."

I stare at the fuzzy blue yarn we're working with and hold the tension with my fingers.

"You're not going out again," she says.

"I'm twenty-seven. You can't really stop me."

She fiddles with the zipper of her purse. "As long as you act like a kid, I'll treat you like one."

"She's twenty-seven," Grandmother says. The yarn slacks around her fingers.

Amma hitches up her purse and storms up the stairs.

Laila Aunty comes by that night. No Appa in sight. Amma is washing dishes and sees Laila Aunty's Lexus pull up in the gravel driveway.

"She's alone," Amma says. She hurriedly wipes her hands on a dishrag and runs up the stairs.

I'm painting on my laptop, coloring over my sketch of the flamenco dancer from *El Jaleo*. Grandmother is knitting a bright red scarf, wavy at the edges where she's dropped and added stitches.

I open the door before Laila Aunty has a chance to knock. She clasps her purse in front of herself. She's wearing a kurta that sparkles when she moves.

"I came to see Grandmother, dear. Is your mother home?"

Amma comes down the stairs. She's changed out of her home clothes and into something she normally wears for work. She and Laila Aunty step around each other on their way to the living room.

Laila Aunty bends down and kisses Grandmother on both

cheeks. Grandmother doesn't seem to know who Laila Aunty is, but she smiles and makes small talk anyway.

Amma sits silently on the sofa. She stares through the sliding glass doors at the vegetable garden that needs weeding.

"How are you, dear?" Laila Aunty asks me. "You must miss Krishna."

I close my laptop. "He'll visit soon."

"Let me make some tea," Amma says.

I start to get up to follow her but she waves me down. She goes to the kitchen.

"Have you drawn anything new?" Laila Aunty asks. "Any pictures of Sri Lanka?"

I've drawn a woman with no arm. I shake my head.

"I wish you'd paint a canvas for us. We need something to hang in the den."

Vidya used to paint for Appa. They still have some of her paintings hanging in their house.

"I'm not that good," I say.

Amma brings tea for each of us.

Laila Aunty takes a sip and closes her eyes. "I miss your tea."

Amma drinks hers in silence.

"At university your mother used to make tea just like this," Laila Aunty says. "Our whole floor would visit our room in the evening instead of going to the cafeteria."

"The cafeteria was very far," Amma says.

"And they only gave plain tea. One of the girls in the hostel had an uncle who had a farm nearby. He brought us milk so we could make tea."

"It's sad what happened to him."

"What happened?" I ask.

Amma wraps her hands around her mug. "He was killed in the riots."

I know about this. The riots that started the Sri Lankan war. I'd read about it in college.

"It was what?" Laila Aunty says. "Third year of university?"

"Third year. We were about to go home for vacation. I had a train ticket for the next morning, but the security guards came to the hostel that night and told us to get to the inner rooms. They had some rooms that were in the middle of the floor that were hard to get to. They said there was a mob heading toward the university."

"News wasn't as easily spread, no. We didn't know that the riots had already started in Colombo."

"They put some Sinhalese boys in charge of protecting us. But some of them wanted revenge, too."

"Some of them threatened us."

"So we took our things and ran."

"We took our tea."

"We did take our tea."

"We went and stayed at this farmer's house, the one that used to give us milk. But the riots spread fast, so we had to move on."

"We couldn't bathe for a week. Remember? It was just a bunch of us girls, no."

"You wouldn't believe the smell."

Amma tucks her legs underneath her and leans forward. Their voices are high-pitched and loud, almost argumentative if you weren't listening to the words.

"We finally found a barn near someone's house that we hid in, but the family found us. It was a nice Muslim family, and they hid us in their daughters' rooms."

"Remember Meena?"

"Meena was a girl on our floor." Laila Aunty lowers her voice. "She had her period during the riots."

"She smelled like you wouldn't believe."

"We snuck her out to the river to wash herself. But when we were bathing—"

"We heard men's voices. We were so scared."

They giggled and wiped at their eyes.

"We snuck off in our wet clothes, hair still wet—"

"Shampoo still on—"

"Eventually the farmer who first took us all in, he arranged for a tractor to take us to Kandy so we could take a bus home."

"They came for him after we left," Laila Aunty says. "They took him out to his field, and burned him."

"Burned all his cattle, too."

"We didn't find out until after we made it back to Jaffna."

Silence rang in the space between their voices.

"So sad," Amma said.

"Our parents were so worried when we got back."

"Your father, too," Amma starts to say. She cuts herself off.

Laila Aunty puts her teacup on the coffee table. It's dainty and ceramic. The tea set for guests.

"Well," she says, standing.

"Thanks for coming."

Laila Aunty starts to move toward Amma but then stops. Instead she kisses Grandmother on the cheeks again and leaves.

When she's gone, Amma washes out her teacup by hand in the sink. She doesn't say anything.

"Why did she come?" I ask.

Amma stops scrubbing the cup. "She has regrets."

That night I dream that I'm on a bus in Sri Lanka, trying to get home to my family. We get stopped at a security checkpoint. While we're all getting searched by army officers, our bus explodes. A woman with no arm falls on me. She shields me from the flames and shrapnel. She's so heavy I can't breathe. I crawl and crawl but she lies on top of me, holding me down.

When I wake up in the middle of the night, I draw the scene. I can't capture the way the woman crushed me, but I can feel it, all over.

It's one of the best sketches I've ever drawn, but it's not what Laila Aunty meant when she said she wanted a painting to hang on her wall.

I go to the rugby house that weekend. I pretend not to hear Amma mutter to herself as she pulls on her gardening gloves and steps outside. Grandmother stands on the deck and holds the railing. I pull on my sneakers and leave before either of them has a chance to say anything.

Tasha and Jesse aren't up when I get there. Tasha's black curls poke out of the rainbow quilt when I knock on the door, and through the open window I see her drag herself to the door.

"Hey you." She leans heavily against the door and wipes her eyes with little squishy sounds.

I follow her inside and throw my duffel bag on the floor next to a pile of Xbox controllers. Someone shifts in her bed. All I can see is a pale forehead.

"I'll make you some coffee." Tasha pushes me into the olive kitchen.

I sit down at the rickety table with mismatched chairs. She putters around the kitchen, pulling coffee and filters from cabinets. The coffee grinder screams a high-pitched wail and the smell of ground coffee fills the room. She makes coffee in a French press, carefully pouring it into two mugs shaped like boobs. She sits down at the table with me.

Black coffee. The mug is yellow with red swirls and a great big red nipple. I'm not a fan of black coffee. I always add sugar and creamer and Amma drinks hers with condensed milk. I blow on it. The air steams up my glasses.

Tasha's already halfway through hers. "I just got these beans." She closes her eyes and breathes in the smell.

"What time are you guys going to practice?"

"Rugby season's over for Boston Women's. Last night was our alumnae game at Wellesley."

I sink further into the chair.

She rubs at her temple, then scratches a tattoo on her neck. "Good thing, too. I think I have a concussion."

"So no rugby."

"Nope. But,"—she holds up a finger—"the MMA tournament is starting."

"MMA?"

"A friend of mine runs it. A bunch of dykes and trans boys fighting in basements for cash. It's terrific."

"Like Fight Club?"

"We don't talk about Fight Club. Want to join?" She reaches out and touches my hair, which is finally long enough to put into a ponytail. "Do you ever think about short hair?"

"I do have short hair."

"I meant shorter. Like mine." She pulls at her curls, stretching one two-inch piece out from her head.

"My mom would kill me."

"You're twenty-something years old. Why the hell are you afraid of your mother?"

She lifts up her hand. I feel the air move around my head before she touches me.

"I've always wanted to cut my hair short," I say.

"Then what are you waiting for?"

Jesse appears around the bend of the hallway. She blinks the sleep out of her eyes and pours herself a cup of coffee. "Are you joining the tournament, Lucky?"

A blond man with high cheekbones stumbles in, his shirt crumpled and his boxers twisted. He looks odd in the house, against the corner of the rainbow flag just above his head.

The man walks to Tasha and puts a hand on her neck. He was the one in her bed earlier. I stare at my coffee and wish it had sugar and cream. I hear him say, "Hey, baby," and something that sounds like a kiss.

Tasha coughs, and when I look up, the man has moved away. He's standing by the fridge, his face crumpling the way that Nisha's does when she's angry.

"I'll call you later," Tasha says to him. "You should probably go."

He wraps his arms around himself and walks into the living room.

"Straight men can be so needy," she says.

When he leaves, Tasha teaches me the basics for the tournament while Jesse watches and plays on her phone.

Tasha rolls up one arm of her T-shirt. "Punch me."

"What?"

"Punch me. Go on." She spreads her legs and tilts toward me. "Go on."

I make a fist and throw my weight at her, unfocused and wobbly.

"Harder. Come on."

I punch again, less wobbly this time.

"Again. Go a little harder each time. Rotate with the motion."

I visualize punching. I picture the muscles in my shoulders, my back twisting back and snapping forward, the power flowing through my arm. I punch again. Again, again, stronger and stronger until Tasha has to widen her stance.

She feels her arm where I just punched. "Not bad, twinkle toes. You may even give me a bruise." She moves behind me and puts her palm flat on my right shoulder blade. "The power comes from here. Rotate with it."

"I was rotating."

She doesn't move her hand from my back. "You can punch a lot harder than this."

"I'm trying."

"Maybe we need to get you angry."

"I'm already angry."

She turns and gives me her other arm to punch. "Not angry enough."

I picture Nisha, her wedding, the way she gets excited about her bridal clothes and how she cried in the car and asked me to run away with her. I haven't heard from her since. I punch, harder and harder, rotating out from my shoulder, again again again.

After a while we have to escape to the deck to let the sweat freeze on our faces. We're all down to our boxer briefs and sports bras.

Tasha makes me chug a bottle of water before handing me a PBR. She tries to convince me to cut my hair.

"Stop pestering her," Jesse says.

"Look at her. She wants to."

I text Kris: *Should I cut my hair?*

He responds: *You hate your hair.*

We gather in the kitchen. Tasha spreads out her buzzer and guards on the table. "Ready?"

I screw my eyes shut. The cold buzzer tickles my head as it runs back and forth, the vibration running through me, slipping down under the pit of my stomach. Hair falls around me. My head feels oddly light. Tasha pulls out scissors and works on the top, biting the tip of her tongue in concentration. Pieces of hair cling to the sweat on my forehead and work their way inside the collar of my T-shirt. Finally, she steps back, throws up her hands and says, "Done." Jesse swats at my back and neck.

My head spins when I stand. I stumble into the bathroom and stop at the mirror. My ears stick out like naked baby birds stretching out their new necks.

Tasha is behind me, arms crossed over her chest. "So? How do you feel, Mulan?"

I rub what's not there on the back of my head. I look like a woman I might stare at from across the room.

My reflection grins.

Tasha's fingernails dance on my neck. "You look good."

By the time I pull up to Amma's doorway, a migraine beats a soft pulse behind my left eyeball. Amma's car is missing, but Nisha's is in our driveway. Nisha opens the door before I have a chance to put my key in the lock. She stands there motionless, her eyes widening slowly.

"Hey." I try a smile. "Can I come in?"

"Your mom's going to kill you." But she's starting to smile. "You're going to be dead for my wedding." She puts a hand on my shoulder and bends down with the force of her laughter. I wonder if she's forgotten about crying, about asking me to run away with her.

Grandmother's in her chair in the living room, watching the TV, blankness stitched on her face. A bit of drool hangs from the side of her mouth. I wipe it off with the hem of my shirt. She turns and looks at me, her eyes blank.

"It's me, Lucky." I take her hand and rub the back of it. "Lucky."

She plucks her hand out of mine and touches the tip of my hair like it's made of glass. "Lucky, you're a boy."

Nisha sits on the edge of the couch armrest and smirks. "You don't look half bad."

"You need to marry her," Grandmother says to me, nodding her head.

"Marry who?"

She doesn't answer. She looks out the sliding doors to the deck. I open the doors so that the musty indoor air can circulate. Grandmother breathes in the wind that rushes in, lets it fill her up. She sits straighter. She's probably been in the chair all afternoon. I should've come home earlier. I'm the only one who helps her walk around when she wants to. I'm the only one who wants her to be strong.

I offer her my arm, and help her stand and hobble to the deck. The weather's unseasonable warmth swirls around us.

Grandmother slowly turns back toward the living room. "I can't hear the baby."

When Amma's car pulls into the driveway, I hide upstairs. Nisha's already left. Grandmother still sits in the living room.

There's the wind chime on the front door. Amma's footsteps. The thunk of her putting her bag down. She says hello to Grandmother.

"Lucky?"

I walk down the stairs, pausing just before I come into view. The next stair feels like stepping off a cliff.

Amma stands at the bottom of the stairs, some mail in her hand. She looks up at me, and freezes. Her mouth hangs open. Her face gets hard, her eyes and lips press together, closer and closer until they're just slits in her face.

"Amma?" My voice is dry and cracked.

She's sinking, her knees giving out under her reaction. She slumps down on the first stair and claws at her chest. The mail drifts to the floor.

I leap down the staircase and kneel next to her. "Amma?" I try to turn her around by the shoulder so I can see her face but she resists.

She sucks in the air around us. Her fingers clutch at her chest. She stares at the carpet.

My fingers tingle with the numbness that threatens to spread. I'm too big for my skin. I did this for a reason. I want this.

I rub circles on her back, hoping to rub out that feeling in my fingers. Around and around, circles, both of us pitching with her crying, trembles and shakes until I can't tell how long we've sat there. Then she sniffs, shrugs my hand off her shoulder, and goes up the stairs without saying a word.

The day I should get my period passes and the safety tampon I put in comes out clean. Every night that white cotton, revealing my panic slice by slice.

Still nothing, I text Kris.

Exciting! he texts back.

I want to tell Tasha, Nisha, someone. I don't even want a baby. I keep my mouth shut.

Nisha talks and talks of running away, but only on the phone. I get text after text of plans: *Toronto. That's where we should go.*

I'm so sick of this wedding. Let's go soon?

I can't wait to wake up next to you every day.

She never gives a date or time, just rising panic. When I see her, she's full of the fake smiles she wore at her engagement. I drag around the cloak of her plans with me wherever I go.

Amma asks me why I'm slouching more than normal. Tasha has to remind me constantly to keep form when I practice for the tournament. I turn corners with these heavy shoulders. Numbness spreads through me again, fills me like cement.

Kris visits on the excuse that he misses me and wants to be with his wife. Amma's delighted. She fawns over him, makes his favorite foods, and tries to prod him along on the path to fatherhood.

He arrives with a bouquet of yellow roses. Unorthodox for a brown man, but he loves to stand out. Amma smiles wide and puts them in water. She hasn't smiled since I cut my hair.

Kris kneels down next to Grandmother in her folding chair. Grandmother turns her head from the afternoon news headlines. *Kerala High Court says buildings of religious groups are taxable. Rogue cop dreams up unique rental business. Richie Ramsay leads at Indian Open.*

Her bluing eyes twitch. "Lucky." She reaches up and touches Kris's hair.

"See?" Amma says. "She doesn't even know the difference between you two anymore." She turns to Kris. "I can't believe you allowed her to cut her hair like this."

Anger folds over inside me.

Kris has a fake smile of his own. "If it makes her happy."

Later, when Amma is busy cooking his favorite shrimp stir-fry, Kris drags me upstairs. "How goes it?" He gives me a look but

I don't know what that's supposed to refer to. Nisha? Tasha? Grandmother?

I sit down on the bed and let him tower over me. My eyelids sag. I droop with the effort of it all. "Fuck if I know."

"That bad?"

I let myself fall backward onto the bed. I hit the mattress with a thump, arms spread wide. My breath leaves me. I watch the slope of the ceiling.

"Your mother's mad at you," he says.

"I know."

"Did you get your period?"

"Nope."

"Can I help?"

"Please don't."

He sits down next to me on the bed. "We fucked this up, didn't we?"

Little canyons run across the sloped ceiling and down the walls, cutting into the plaster.

"We should be happy," he says. "We did this to be happy."

"Maybe it just wasn't in the stars for us." I'm starting to sound like Amma. Rewriting your fate is tricky. We get to keep our families, but we lose something in return. The law of equivalent exchange.

Amma takes me aside that evening while Kris works in the back-yard, harvesting the last of the cabbage from Amma's garden. The only time he gets his hands dirty is when he's playing the good brown husband.

I watch him from the living room, his thin back bent over the patch of dirt, his spine visible through his striped polo, his long shadow mixing in with the others as the sun goes down.

"He's a good man," Amma says. She clears her throat. She does that every time she talks to Laila Aunty. She's going to say something she doesn't want to say. "How are you with money?" she asks.

I count the stripes on Kris's polo. Seven. "Fine."

"Grandmother's hospital bills are getting out of hand. I—I need help with them." She stares out the sliding glass doors, not meeting my eyes.

"Of course I'll help." For the first time there's something I can give her. Money is power. A chance to turn the tables. I don't think she even knows what she's given me. I may have lost in my battle with fate, but I haven't lost to Amma quite yet.

———

Kris isn't so sure. "We just don't have that much lying around." He keeps his voice low so that Amma, sleeping in the guest bedroom, won't hear.

"We've been saving." I lie down next to him in the bed and bump his shoulder with mine. "Amma needs this."

"I'm not actually an engineer, you know. I don't make nearly as much as your mother thinks I do. And you can barely contribute with your commissions."

"I contribute."

"This is our nest egg, Lucky. If we give it to her, we have nothing."

"We have equity on the house. I'll get a job. A real job."

"You've tried. There are no jobs in this damn recession."

I bend his index finger back until it cracks. "I'll apply again." Then his middle finger. Then his ring finger. "I'll keep applying." I crack his pinky.

He yanks his hand away.

"I'll fucking work at McDonald's if I have to," I say.

"I'm not giving her the money." He turns his head away from me and draws the blankets tighter around himself.

"You don't make these decisions. I could apply for a divorce."

"And be the divorced gay daughter? Your mom wouldn't even want your money then."

"And you'll have to go back to India. How does that sound?"

"You wouldn't."

"She needs this money." I tug on his arm until he turns around. "It's my fault that Grandmother was in the hospital. We have to pay."

His eyes follow me even when I look away. I get up and change into my boxers for bed. Amma's decided to give us privacy, so I can at least sleep how I want to.

"Fine." Kris stabs a finger at me. "But you get a job."

~

I visit Nisha on the weekends, and her parents take us to temple. I follow her around the shrines. Sometimes she stops so suddenly I run into her. She turns back coyly. She drags me to the bathroom. She tries to feed me lemon rice from her plate. I watch her parents carefully, just in case they notice. I'm wary of smiling too big or sitting too close.

One time when I go to her house, she's alone. She giggles when she opens the door. "They're gone." She looks around behind me and pulls me inside. She has no makeup on and she's still in her pajamas. "I told them I had my period."

Women during their periods are considered unclean. In the past they weren't allowed to cook or even enter the kitchen. Now we're just not allowed to go to temple or pray. Progress, according to Amma.

Nisha pulls me by the hand up the curved staircase. The picture of her at her puberty ceremony looms over me as I climb, her face still full—baby-fat cheeks, too-big teeth and no lines. Menstruating women are unclean, but when a girl reaches menarche, we throw a party.

Inside Nisha's bedroom, the menagerie of stuffed animals watches me. One side of her mouth curls up. She looks at the bed, then back at me. I like the depth of her face without makeup, the shadows and bumps that haven't been hidden away. She pulls her shirt off, unbuckles her bra and walks toward me.

She takes my hands and puts them on her chest. I run my thumbs over her puckered nipples. She makes me sit on the bed and straddles my lap.

"It's not really cheating if you're not really married," she says.

Her thighs press against my jeans. She puts her nipple in my mouth and rubs herself off on my leg. I have a tampon in, just in case. My period is three weeks late, but I've always been erratic when stressed. She won't try to touch me. I stay clothed. I suck on her nipple and scratch down her back. She bites my neck. I reach down and finger her and let her ride me. I'm the one not really married, so I'm the one not really cheating. Her marriage will be real. I wonder if she'll hold onto his biceps and arch against him and muffle her moans against his neck. He'll have to learn how to pull her hair the way she likes. When she comes she bites so hard she draws blood.

Afterward, we lie on her bed—the same bed we bounced on as kids, the one where she painted my nails during sleepovers, where we pulled the covers up to our chins to tell each other ghost stories. I hold her and feel my eyes close with the weight that follows me. I'm not the one cheating, but I'm the one who feels the burden.

A scream wakes us. Nisha's mother. My arm's numb from hours of Nisha's sleeping form.

Nisha scrambles to cover herself with the blanket. She yanks it out from under me and I fall to the floor. My tailbone lands hard on the wood.

Nisha's mother runs across the room, shrieking too loud for her petite, withering body. I only catch a few words. Tamil falls too fast and shrill. Nisha stands mummified in her blankets. She's taller than her mother but seems tiny.

Nisha's mother pulls back her arm, twists, and swings the slap from her shoulder. She doesn't stop, her hand slamming across Nisha's face, sharp crisp thuds that hang in the air.

I jump up and lunge forward, catch the hand that swings a wild pendulum. Her eyes bulge, her mouth edged with spittle.

She shoves me hard. I stagger. She shrieks, calls me something I don't understand, waits with wide eyes and when I don't move—

"Get out."

I stumble into Nisha's father at the top of the stairs. He pushes his thick glasses up and looks away, stares hard at the wall. I stomp fast down the stairs and out the door, running run run until I can't see the house. My heart won't slow. My hands shake with cold. I have no coat. I left my car.

I can't go to Amma's house. Nisha's mother may have already called her. I walk to a bus stop and wait, shivering. In the gray sidewalk I see Nisha's face, caught in the back and forth momentum of her mother's hand. The bus pulls up and I ride it to the end of its route.

As the bus pulls into the T station, my phone rings. Amma. "Hello?"

Silence on the line.

I get off the bus and walk down to the platform. "Hello? Amma?"

"What did you do, Lucky?"

"I didn't—"

"Be quiet."

That tone, like in college. Last time led to me being homeless, to Tim, to Kris, to my wedding. A hand swinging wildly across Nisha's face.

"Nisha's father called," Amma says.

I've swallowed sand. I wait.

I'm not alone on the platform. An older man, no more than a mass of dirty clothes, slumps on the wall under an ad for Maui, his sleepy head nodding off near the bikini breast cups of the model. A punk kid sits on the bench next to me, his eyes scrunched up underneath thick glasses, his blue head bent over a Harry Potter book.

Amma's waiting for my explanation. Cold air rushes from the tunnel.

"Amma. I didn't do—"

"I told you to be quiet." Her voice is strangled, a cold whisper that makes me want to drop the phone.

The whooshing rumble of the Orange Line fills the station.

"Amma, please."

"Come home. Now."

"But—"

"It's your choice," she says.

Amma has hung up, or I've lost the signal. The train doors open. I enter the empty car.

THE LAST LIE

By the time I step off the T in JP, I'm shaky. I want to giggle, roll on the floor and pound my fists on the linoleum of the station until my knuckles bleed. I walk through the park where we played rugby. A breeze carries smells of Chinese fish fry. I sit on the bench to think. I didn't tell Tasha or Jesse that I was coming, didn't ask if they minded. I swung myself from Nisha's house and this is where I landed.

A father tries to teach his daughter to walk on the grass. The kid stumbles after a couple of steps and freezes on her hands and knees until the father stands her up again. Appa taught me how to walk by putting my feet on his and stepping with me. Bikers pedal by, their hippie cotton skirts lifted up by the wind of their own movement. I taught myself how to ride a bike.

Sitting still makes me cold. I walk to the rugby house. I don't know if I can tell them. I don't want their pity, don't want to be told it gets better. My parents are the kind of people who talk politics but never mention gay marriage, who watch the news but change the channel at the mention of gayness. Shame, dishonor, embarrassment. Five hundred Sri Lankan Tamil families in the greater Boston area, and not one of them has a gay kid.

Tasha and Jesse are smoking on the deck when I get to the rugby house.

"Hey handsome." Jesse waves. "You okay?"

I twist away, watch the sparse trees that line the sidewalk. Tasha holds out a cigarette and I take it, lighting it from the one in Tasha's mouth.

By the third cigarette, I'm restless. My legs are asleep. I can't get the sinking feeling out of my stomach, a physical pain every time I look at my phone and see that no one has called.

I suggest rugby, and Jesse calls up some people they know in the neighborhood. A half hour later we're in the park, lining up for a scrum. I want to run and fight and fuck, anything to quiet the static in my head. We line up five on five. Jesse plays a hooker as always, built dense and strong to power through the scrum. I line up next to her as the loosehead prop, snake my hands into her shirt and ball them up in her sports bra for leverage. We push push push and the ball peeks from under our line.

As we play I gasp cold air. The stinging wakes me up. My legs hurt. My mouthguard tastes like toothpaste. When we ruck or fall down in tackles the other girls smell like dirt and grass. Their sweat coats my skin.

I get tackled to the ground three times, landing harder and harder on my back and tailbone. I still can't tackle well. Legal tackle means cheek to cheek, the side of your face on her butt.

It means knowing how to fall forward, how to lose balance on purpose, how to drive something home.

We play until it's too dark, and for a moment, with the sun dipping under the trees and the leaves crunching under our steps, Tasha's arm over my shoulder, and the clink of twelve-packs from the liquor store, just for a moment I can forget.

Amma doesn't call. I keep waiting for the phone to ring, check it every five minutes like a tick, turn up the ringer when I go to bed, but still nothing.

I lie next to Tasha in the living room. My stomach twists and spirals, keeps me awake. My heart beats too fast to settle down for sleep. I feel Tasha next to me. We don't touch but the air between us presses warm against me. A subtle shift when she turns under the sheets. The mattress dips in the middle. I want to let myself roll into her. My muscles tense up trying not to.

I wake up on my side, arms spilling over the edge of the bed. I'm sore. The backs of my knees ache and my tailbone is tender. Tasha is inches away.

Through the doorway to the kitchen, Jesse makes something on the stove. A girl I haven't seen before, a petite brunette drowning in one of Jesse's jerseys, rummages in the fridge. I get out of bed and join them.

"Want some eggs, you?" Jesse asks. "You need to bulk up. It'll help your game." She sprays some oil onto a skillet. Gray, thick smoke shoots out from the pan. She breaks five eggs into it. Crackling fills the kitchen.

The brunette watches me, frowning at the tips of her mouth.

When I look at her, she looks away. She kisses Jesse. Nisha's absence is lodged in between my lungs. There isn't enough air. The exposed wood beams are siphoning oxygen into the October winds outside. I hold onto the doorframe.

"I'm going to take a walk," I say.

Jesse flips over the mass of eggs. She calls after me as I leave. "Feel free to grab something in the fridge."

I step out into the clear morning air. I should've worn a coat. I put my hands in my pockets and walk down the creaky steps to the sidewalk. The sky spreads a clear blue, the air crisp and unmoving. I walk toward the park. A young woman my age pushes a stroller. An old man in a motorized wheelchair holds a small poodle on his lap. Garden blooms, the last of the fall, bend toward me from the retaining walls that hold in people's yards. I check my phone. No calls. What if Amma never calls me back? What if Nisha never talks to me again? I call Kris, but the phone rings and rings and goes to voice mail.

I jog the rest of the way to the T station and climb down the stone steps. People lumber around the station, holding whimpering babies to their chests and adjusting diaper bags. Too many people. Amma's never going to call back. Bile rises at the back of my throat. I have to be the one to do it. I have to go back to Amma's house.

The tiled walls grumble as the train arrives, but I've left my Charlie Card at the rugby house.

⌒

Tasha's up and out of bed, sitting on the crumpled sheets playing Xbox when I walk in. She pats the space next to her.

I want to crawl back into bed and sleep until my lungs can expand without pain. I sit down.

"Did you guys have a fight?" Tasha asks. "You and Nisha?"

"Yeah, yeah we had a fight."

She sucks in air through her teeth. In the morning light, her broken-and-glued-back-together tooth shines. The jagged edge of it glows dark and clear.

I spin my wedding ring around and around on my finger.

She offers me a game controller. "Plenty of fish in the sea."

The longer I wait to go back to Amma's house, the harder it'll be. I should walk back down to the station, step onto a train, go back home. My legs refuse to move. I fall back onto the couch.

"Stay for a while." Tasha pats my knee and places the controller on my lap.

"I don't want to overstay my welcome."

"Nonsense."

We play for a while in silence. She pauses the game, goes to the kitchen and comes back with two IPAs. "Stay the week, then go. It'll be fun."

I drink my beer fast. One week in the rugby house.

She punches me in the arm and un-pauses the game, smiling with her broken tooth.

⌒

We go to a string of parties with drunk people I don't know. The first is a block party in the rugby house neighborhood. Young professionals and parents, small kids and large dogs. A table struggles under food—everything from curry to steak to sushi. There are other South Asians there—young, hip couples who ignore me and a couple of new immigrant men who stare.

One of the Indian men keeps his eyes on me from across the party. He is light skinned and doughy, the kind of man Amma finds attractive. I talk to an older man about his work certifying organic farms for the government. I coo over a woman's German shepherd that she's taught to stand on its hind legs and hug people. I keep up a string of conversations because every time I get done talking, the man looks like he's going to come over. After a while I look for Tasha and Jesse. The Indian man heads my way. His face would be kind if he wasn't leering, his sharp eyes focused on me like there's no one else in the world.

"Do I know you?" he asks.

I try for the most uninviting look I can manage. "I don't think so."

"I think our parents were friends."

"I don't think so."

He tries to laugh and ends up scowling. His forehead gets extra shiny with sweat. "But you're from India?"

"Sri Lanka."

"Yes, yes, Sri Lanka." He looks down at his paper plate and takes a bite of fufu. He chews it for a long time, and swallows with difficulty. "These Americans with their bland food. I miss my mother's cooking. Do you cook?"

"Fufu is African food. You're supposed to eat it with soup."

"I came here for my studies. I just got a job at a good company. Do you go to school?"

I catch sight of Jesse near the food table, holding hands with her girlfriend. The Indian man looks at them. Jesse pulls her girlfriend in for a kiss.

"They are so shameless." He turns back to me and gives me an embarrassed smile, as if we share some secret.

I think of Nisha, of her mother's hand whipping across her face.

"Hey you," Tasha says into my ear. She looks at the Indian man and takes a step closer to me.

He chokes on his rice. He opens his mouth, but when no sound comes out, he closes it.

She pulls on my shoulder, nods at the man, and leads me away.

⁓

Tasha takes me canvassing door to door for the Obama campaign. Two weeks until the election. We walk up and down the steep hills of JP until my calves ache. I carry a clipboard and wear a campaign shirt, but I don't know the spiel so I stand back near the curb and let Tasha talk to disgruntled voters. Their eyes pass over her shirt. They nod and shut the door.

"Is anyone in JP not voting for Obama?" I ask.

"You have a point. But I agreed to do this neighborhood." She scratches the side of her leg and squints against the sun. She looks down at her clipboard of names.

We keep walking. Dried leaves litter the street.

She stops halfway up a hill and looks around. "Did we do this street already?"

It doesn't look familiar, but we've walked through so many I can't keep track. "Ring a doorbell and see if you recognize someone."

"All these white people look the same to me. I can't tell."

We start to climb again. She looks down at her clipboard

and rings a doorbell. I stand on the sidewalk while she talks to an older lady holding a tabby cat.

She crosses a name off her clipboard. "Two more streets." She's quiet for a while. "I know it's not my business, but I'm sorry about Nisha."

The air fills with fall chill.

"I know it can't be easy with your family," she says.

"Are you close with yours?" I don't know anything about Tasha's family. She never talks about them.

"My family stopped talking to me when they found out I was queer." She kicks a pile of leaves pressed up against the curb, and they flutter out from her feet and scatter on the road. "So I get it."

My voice jumps ahead of my thoughts. "My sister ran away from home after college. I haven't talked to her since."

"Have you tried to find her?"

"I don't think she wants to be found."

Tasha checks the clipboard again and starts walking.

"I was such a dick to my family," she says.

"It's never too late."

She stops mid-stride. "At some point I realized I couldn't save anyone but myself. So I stopped trying."

She keeps walking and I follow.

One night after rugby, we buy Captain Morgan and craft beer. Jesse and Tasha call up other friends, and we sing rugby songs and play cards. During our smoke breaks the cold air can't touch me, and when Tasha puts her fingers on my cheeks and kisses me, I pull her closer by the waist and kiss her back.

Vidya's letter rests in a pocket of the jeans I've worn since Nisha's house, folded neatly along the already-existing crease in the paper and tucked back in the envelope with the photo. At night I take out the envelope, run my thumb over the serrated edges of the American flag stamp, follow the blocky white text underneath it—Liberty—the return address in Louisville, Kentucky, written in Vidya's scrawl. I read over the tall loopy writing, the short, square note framed on each side by thick white space. I stare at the photo of Vidya and her daughter, the little girl's black curls frozen in a bounce, her chubby hands reaching out toward me. Vidya's skirt blows around her slim hips, her face still the prettiest of us all. She's smiling at someone. Jamal behind the camera? I want to think so, believe that she ran away for a reason that lasted. Maybe I just want to believe that Amma was wrong.

Before I go to bed I slip the paper and photo back in the envelope and settle it back in my pocket. Louisville, Kentucky. A sixteen-and-a-half hour drive. Fifteen hours if I drive above the speed limit, and I always do.

—

I finally decide to tell them. Tasha and Jesse gather around me and listen to the story. The whole story, Nisha's parents catching us, Amma's phone call, everything. I'm done lying to them.

"I'm going to go back home soon." Just the thought of that cluttered house with all of Kris's depression littered around makes me weary.

Tasha puts down her beer and puts her hand on my knee. "We like having you around."

At night, I lie in Tasha's bed and think about Grandmother doubled over with the coughs, her eyes blank with bluish haze. Who is getting her water now? Is Amma taking leave from work?

I take out Vidya's letter and carry it to the porch. A few lights dot the otherwise empty street. A clear fall moon hangs in the sky. I can smell the cold in the air now, the winter moving in too late. When we were younger, Vidya always wanted to be outside. She thrived in nature while Shyama sat inside with the AC and the cleanliness of Amma's housekeeping. Vidya and I ran around the neighborhood climbing trees and getting dirt under our fingernails that Amma would painfully dig out later with a safety pin.

What would Vidya say? In college, when Amma stopped talking to me, it was Vidya who smoothed things over, Vidya who drove out to bring me home, Vidya who tried to talk me out of marrying Kris, Vidya who kept my secrets safe. Louis-ville, Kentucky. A fifteen-hour drive.

After the incident with Kris's roommate in college, I spent the rest of the semester living in the prop room of the theatre building. The attic smelled like history, like memories that didn't belong to me, sleeping thick among the shelves of liquor bottles and kitchen props. There were large Chippendale chaises and flower chandeliers from the seventies, typewriters and rows of chairs of all shapes. I did my homework curled into the arm of an enormous mustard leather wing chair. When I got bored, I browsed the stacks of weapons or the collection of old books—illustrated kid's editions of *Moby Dick* and *Robinson Crusoe*, 1950s housekeeping manuals, dusty copies of Anaïs Nin's diaries. There was an old shortwave radio that worked.

The place had a reputation for being haunted. Students and maintenance staff ignored the creaks I made, the unex-plained music. When students came up to get props, I hid behind old electronics in the back of the attic. I slept on piles of pillows.

Kris brought me food from the cafeteria, and I hid it with the other pantry items, between Snowdrift vegetable shortening and Tony Chachere's red beans and rice.

When it got too hot, I found fans to cool me off. Exploring was enough to take my mind off not having a home. I showered in the gym. Sometimes I fucked girls so that I could sleep in a real bed. And sometimes, when things got bad, I would think about Kris's offer to get married. I was on track to graduate that summer, and then what? The economy was tanking, and what if I couldn't get a job? The longer I lived in that attic, the saner his idea seemed.

~

Tasha and I drive out in the midafternoon in her Kia. I take off my shoes and brace my feet above the glove box. With every left turn, her fuzzy rainbow dice and college graduation tassel—both slung on the rearview mirror—tickle my feet. She plays old CDs while we drive, and sings to Disney songs as the car winds around the long blue Adirondacks. I have Vidya's letter in my shirt pocket.

From the sides of the highway, trees bend toward the road like they're going to scoop us up in their foliage. We chase the slice of clear blue sky that cuts through the tree line. Here and there, a water tower floats above the forest that blankets the mountains and obscures the villages. We drive blind, our future in the hands of the mountains that reveal the next slice of road around the bend.

In a valley town we take an exit to get fast food burgers and fries. Tasha insists that she doesn't allow eating in her car, so we sit on a park bench.

"You know," she says, contemplating a curly fry with a frown, "Nisha's a good person."

I slump my shoulders and hope she notices.

She bites into her burger and wipes her mouth on her sleeve. "You and Nisha. How serious was it?"

"I never expected us to grow old together."

She watches the empty park—about the size of a soccer field, littered with trees. A swing set and a single rusty slide. "You want to work on your tackles?"

"Now?"

She crunches up the burger wrappings and drops them into a trashcan. "Why not?"

I don't have an answer, so we walk to the middle of the grassy area, clear the ground of sticks and glass, and face each other.

She pulls up her plaid cargo pants. "You know the basics. Cheek to cheek. Below the waist."

She runs at me before I can prepare myself. Her arms make contact with my pelvis and the world tips. I land with a thud that knocks the air out of me. She lands on top of me, scrambles up, and helps me to my feet.

In slow motion, she squats and tips herself forward, clasping her arms behind my butt. Her head rests on the side of my hip. "This is the ideal position you want. You try."

I bend down to her pelvis and wrap my arms around her. Musty laundry and cologne. I should be used to her smell by now. It gets inside my nose and stays there. I can taste her when I breathe out.

"Now push with your legs," she says. "Not with your back. Keep your back straight and drive your legs forward, up and forward."

Back straight. Know how to fall. Hold onto something, and drive it to the ground. I push with all my strength and her knees buckle. We fall into a heap. I land on my hands.

She knocks my arms out with her elbows. I fall heavily onto her.

"Always land on your opponent. It knocks the air out of them." Her arms wind around my waist and hold me there.

I nod and she lets me up. We knock each other down a few more times until I work up to doing a running tackle. I get used to the feeling of her hips, the momentary vertigo, the fall.

"Squeeze me tight to you. Clasp your arms together. Don't leave an opening."

I run at her and drive her to the ground.

Her head is cradled in the un-mowed grass. "Always look at the person. Never look at the ground." She hooks a leg behind my knees and flips us so that I'm pinned underneath her.

"Never look at the ground."

She's thinking about kissing me. I can see it in her eyes. She stays like that for a few minutes, raised slightly on her elbows, her curls plastered to her head with sweat, before jumping up and heading toward the car.

∼

The mountains crack open into hills, and again into flatter land. The sky stretches further, wider, shows off a few stars, faint against the well-lit highway. We switch off driving every three hours. By midnight my eyes hurt. My muscles, saturated with coffee, spasm at the stillness. A group of thirty motorcycles passes us, some of the men doing wheelies and shouting into our car. Tasha stirs from her nap. I keep driving.

We stop at a Super 8 off the highway at two in the morning. The Indian attendant at the desk stares at me. It's late. I'm here with a black girl who clearly looks like a lesbian. And with this hair, I probably look like a lesbian, too.

∼

I wake up bleeding. Blood smears between my thighs. My boxers are soaked. I jump out of bed in a panic. The sheets are clean except for a quarter-sized spot of red. I've waited for my period so long that I stopped putting a tampon in. Finally. A month late. Finally.

Tasha's already up, drinking coffee from a Styrofoam cup. She looks at the sheets. "It's not so bad. They'll bleach it."

I wash my boxers in the bathroom sink but the blood won't come out.

The Indian attendant is still there when we check out. He stares with that same look, like he's watching a bad car wreck.

"That guy certainly has eyes for you," Tasha says in the car. She goes through a box of CDs and picks out the soundtrack to Disney's *A Goofy Movie*.

I toe off my shoes and prop my feet back up on the dash. Sunlight filters through the gray clouds, taking on their smoky, dusty feel by the time it lands on my skin. Tasha bobs her head up and down to the music and puts Vidya's address into her phone's GPS. I force my breath to slow and deepen, and try not to pay attention to the cramps sparking in my abdomen.

She drops the phone into a cup holder. An electronic voice drones on to take the next available U-turn. Tasha sings along with the tape. I clench my teeth through the pain. We drive.

After the spring college semester ended, I didn't go home. Kris and I both stayed in the prop room, preparing for graduation and applying for jobs. Vidya called me every day. I only answered when I thought I could lie effectively. One day she called four times in a row. When I finally picked up, she said, "Where are you?"

"I'm at home."

"I'm at your apartment. Where are you?"

"You're here? Who's with you?"

"It's just me. Where are you?"

"I just got out of class."

"I'll come and get you."

Back then I needed time to prepare my lies. I gave her directions to the building where some summer classes were held. I stood out on the curb with my backpack. A riot of petals lay crushed on the sidewalk, the air sweet with their smell. Vidya pulled up and I climbed quietly into the passenger seat. She sat with the car in park, silent.

"Why are you here?" I asked. My teeth chattered but not with cold.

"I'm here to take you home."

"I can't."

She turned around in her seat. "Amma needs to see you, talk to you."

"She doesn't want to see me."

A class had just gotten out. The sidewalk filled with students. She stroked my hair. "Amma wants to see you. I talked to her." She turned my face to her.

"I love you the same, Lucky."

I tried to keep it in but I cried anyway.

"Amma will too, eventually," she said. She put both hands back on the steering wheel. "Back to your apartment?"

"I—just the theatre building." I gave her directions.

"I didn't know there were dorms in the theatre building."

I dried my face with my sleeves and didn't correct her.

⁓

I wake up in Louisville. Tasha shakes my arm. I stretch my legs by walking them up the sun-warmed windshield.

Louisville is too bright. The air conditioning blows tepid and dusty against my arms. Sunlight rushes around the car. I squint against it, using my hand for shade. We pass a baseball stadium near an overpass. Great cracks run through the highway, patched over with tar.

We drive into a small cluster of city-like buildings, all gray steel and blue-green glass. Buildings flash by in a whirl of brick. A large poster of Muhammad Ali watches us from a concrete museum. A scooped-out façade of a building rises on a road by the shore. The Ohio River blinks at us through the empty windows.

"Destination on your right," the GPS says. The blue of the river unfolds on Tasha's side of the car. Metal sculptures dot the wide sidewalks of Main Street. People in business suits swarm on the sidewalks, women in too-small skirts, men in pinstripe and Windsor knots. I can't imagine Vidya among these too-clean people, her ruffled skirts and her wild hair.

The building the GPS leads us to is dark brick with white Grecian trim, an Italian restaurant and a couple of boutique stores on the first floor.

I wipe my sweaty palms on my jeans.

"Where the hell are we supposed to park?" Tasha swings the car right, up a hill, past fancy hotels.

Vidya's building is shrinking, sliced by the defroster grid

of the car's back window. Tasha pats my knee. The concrete runs seamless down the buildings, across the streets and up the other side.

We find a parking garage with water-stained cement floors. Our sneakers squeak on it, even after we get onto dry concrete. I crack my knuckles one by one. The tips of my fingers have lost all warmth. Upright, I can feel the blood falling inside me. It magnifies in my head.

Tasha bumps my shoulder with hers, winds her arm around mine and weaves our fingers together. My palms sweat but she doesn't flinch away.

We walk to Vidya's building faster than I expect. Our palms are plastered together with sweat. I shake mine out of her grasp to let the air in.

Outside the building, two intertwining bodies make a bright orange metal sculpture. I squint at it, trying to make out where one form ends and the other begins. It's familiar, the shape of the sculpture, but I can't think of why.

The glass doors of the building open into a circular lobby. Grass-textured walls wind close on all sides. We get in the gilded elevator and watch the floor fall away. Fourth floor. A blank wall and a hallway carpeted with crimson filigree like a twenties hotel. Vidya's door is glossy black like all the others, six paneled with a peephole and a tarnished gold knocker with the face of a lion. Apartment 429. I lift the knocker's circular handle and let it fall down onto the door. We wait.

I knock again. We wait.

Eventually Tasha knocks at number 428. Nothing. I knock at number 427. The door opens. A little kid with a round, broad face pops his head around the door, hiding.

"Do you know who lives in this apartment?" Tasha points to Vidya's door.

The little kid looks at the carpet and nods.

"Do you know where they are?"

He looks at Vidya's door, then at us, and shuts the door. Tasha knocks again. A woman opens the door and hangs her head out into the hallway.

"Do you know where the people in apartment four twenty-nine are?"

"Why do you want to know?"

I step forward. "I'm her sister."

The woman looks me up and down. "You don't look like her sister."

"We look a lot alike. She has longer hair, curly." I show her the picture that came with the letter.

The woman takes the photo. I want to snatch it back.

"This woman hasn't lived here in years. She moved out with her little girl."

"Where did she go?"

"She said something about Pennsylvania." The woman taps her finger on her chin. "I may not be remembering right."

The blood has fallen away from my fingers, leaving me empty. Tasha grabs my hand and puts her fingers through mine. She thanks the woman and pulls me toward the elevator. I follow, grinding my shoes into the carpet so that they squeak.

Outside, I blink into the sun and trace the lines of the orange sculpture again, trying to find the point of separation between the two forms. Tasha pulls out a cigarette and lights it. She walks around and around the sculpture, taking puffs of smoke and blowing it around the metal.

"What now?" she asks.

"I guess we go back."

She stands near the sculpture's plaque for a long time. She takes a drag from the cigarette and throws it down. "Come here and look at this."

The town of Louisville proudly sponsors The Living Art Walk. Title: "The Lovers." Artist: Vidya Jeyakumar.

I reach up and press my hand to the metal. It's warm, the orange paint starting to pucker and bubble.

Vidya Jeyakumar. She never changed her name.

"Why would she put this address on a letter if she doesn't live here anymore?" I ask.

"The city hall will have records of the artists who contributed," Tasha says. "They may have a current address on file."

But they don't. All they have is the address in Louisville. I can't feel the blood inside me. Vidya is good at disappearing, but I don't know what she's running from anymore.

～

When Vidya came to get me from college and brought me home to Amma, she asked me why I didn't tell her.

"Tell you what?" I fiddled with the zipper on my backpack.

"Tell me what happened with Amma."

"I didn't know how you felt about—you know."

She stared straight ahead at the lines of the curving highway and blinked rapidly. "I'm your sister."

"Still."

"It doesn't change anything," she said.

"Does Shyama know?"

"No."

"Don't tell her." I pressed my forehead against the cold window. I couldn't talk around the fear in my throat.

"It's not a terrible thing, Lucky."

I swallowed down the lump. "Amma will never accept this."

"She has to change."

"She won't." I turned my face so she couldn't see me cry. "She stopped transferring me money. I've been living in the prop room."

Vidya slowed and stopped the car on the side of the road. She pulled me to her and held me. Her hands shook. I felt her crying on my scalp.

I hoped that Amma would've gone to bed by the time we made it to Winchester, but the lights were on and through the kitchen window I saw her making sambol. She pounded dried peppers, onions, and coconut shavings in a stone mortar.

Vidya took my duffel bag and unlocked the front door. I stayed in the car.

She dropped my bag off inside and came back out. "You can't stay in there forever."

"Watch me."

"I promise you I won't leave your side." I remember Vidya said that then, though neither of us could've known that she'd be gone by the end of the year.

I couldn't make myself move. She grabbed a handful of my T-shirt and pulled me out. I couldn't make myself resist.

I walked in the door and into the kitchen. Amma froze for a moment, her back tense. For a second no one moved. Then Amma hunched her shoulders and scraped the sambol out of the mortar.

I stepped forward. I couldn't breathe. "Amma." I had

prepared a speech during the ride, everything I wanted to say. But no words came to me in the too bright kitchen, cold vinyl floor under my feet. "Amma."

"This isn't something she can control," Vidya said. "You have to accept this."

Amma put the sambol aside and cut into a fresh onion.

"Amma, talk to her. Please."

Amma's grip on the knife loosened. Her cutting stilled. "I can't accept a daughter like this."

Something was rising in my throat. I swallowed it down.

"This is no kind of life," Amma said.

"This is a perfectly fine kind of life," Vidya said. Her voice rose. She was going to fight for me. But I didn't want to fight anymore. I didn't want to live in the prop room and I didn't want to walk away.

"Amma," I said. "I want to marry Kris. I love him."

On the way back to Boston from Louisville, I get a short and clipped phone call from Amma, her voice scratchy under bad reception in the mountains.

"Come home." Her voice sounds hollow, like she isn't really there.

I lose reception as we drive, chased by a knife-thin moon. I could go back to her house. Or I could walk away, cover my tracks, disappear. I hold my face in my hands and breathe in the wet blackness around me, my body too heavy, a balloon filled with water, dragging me down, crushing me into the seat of the car.

Nisha finally calls that night, after we get back to the rugby house and just as I'm getting ready to pass out. She doesn't answer right away when I say hello. Silence stretches and stretches on the line.

"Hello?" I cup the phone to block out the sound of Tasha and Jesse playing *Guitar Hero*. I walk outside onto the porch and shut the door. The night chill wraps around me. "Hello?"

A sniff. More silence.

"If you don't answer, I'll hang up," I say.

Another sniff.

"Nisha."

"Take me away from here." Her voice tight like a violin string. "Please."

"What do you want me to do?"

"You said we'd go somewhere."

Through the window, the rugby girls are still playing. My absence is unnoticed.

"You said we'd go," Nisha says.

"Now?"

She makes angry sounds, none of them actual words. "You said. You promised."

Jesse hollers her victory dance.

"You promised."

"Okay, okay. Okay. We'll go."

"Tomorrow?"

"Tomorrow. Meet me at Alewife at ten."

Her voice breaks, halting. "Thank you."

I stay out on the deck after I put away my phone. The cold

from the creaky floorboards soaks into my feet. The moon lights the deck in blue.

I can't take Nisha to Toronto like she wants. But I can take her to Bridgeport, to my house. Kris will understand. Her parents won't find her there.

The wind feels new, but then again Boston wind always feels new, solid and pregnant with the sea. Windows glow stark yellow against the painted blue of the buildings. Alewife at ten. Tomorrow everything will change, or maybe it's already changed, and I'm just waiting for it to sprout like spring growth. Tomorrow I'll bring Nisha home, and she'll belong to no one.

Eight o'clock. My alarm bounces off the walls of the rugby house and echoes inside my head. No one is up this early. Tasha moans a complaint and pulls the rainbow quilt over her face. I dive for my phone and shut off the alarm. I want to sink into the mattress. I massage the sleep out of my eyes and swing my feet over the edge of the bed.

"Where are you going?" Tasha's voice is muffled by the quilt.

"Back home."

"This early?"

I roll my shoulders to get some feeling into them, but even that takes an enormous amount of effort. "I'm getting old."

She rolls over and pokes me in the side, where love handles are starting to form. "Don't forget to come back."

I want to tell her about Nisha but I can't find the words.

Eight twenty-three. When I get changed and out of the bathroom, Tasha's in the kitchen.

"Coffee." She gives me the boob cup. "I put milk and sugar in it."

I let the coffee slide down my throat. Beer might be a better start to the day. Whiskey. It would still my fingers.

She flips pancakes on the stove, adds one to a short stack and brings the plate over.

I sit down and pour maple syrup over them. "You didn't have to do all this."

"I always cook for girls who stay the night. I figured you'd need your strength to face your family." She cuts a piece of my pancake stack and puts it in her mouth.

My fingers clamp on the fork and cut large, messy pieces.

Nine forty-seven. I take the T from JP to Alewife, walk up out of the concrete building, and sit on the bench where smokers mill about. The sun slants under the roof of the parking garage and warms the tops of my shoulders, working the tension out. I smell cold in the air, but the nip isn't strong enough for a winter jacket.

A curvy woman in a business suit smokes in her stilettos, flicking the cigarette repeatedly and squinting up at the sky. "Hope this heatwave lasts," she says to me.

I want to feel the cold air around me. This chill is too mild for the end of October. I want the trees to crust over with frost, to see Boston dusted with white before Thanksgiving like when I was a kid.

The woman stamps the cigarette with a pointy-toed shoe. She squints at the sky again, her hand shielding her face, and walks down the steps to the trains.

Ten o'clock. I watch the time on my phone. It gets hard to swallow or breathe.

Ten fifteen. Nisha is late. I send her texts, try to call. Her phone is out of service. She's supposed to be bringing my car.

Ten thirty-two. I walk around to get the feeling back into my legs, and sit down again next to a homeless man in a dirty, torn military jacket who keeps wiping at his nose with his sleeve. He ignores me.

Eleven forty-four. Nisha isn't coming. She's not coming. Traffic wouldn't be this bad on a Sunday. Her phone is still out of service.

I kick at a trashcan. The homeless man stares at me, wiping at his nose. I sit back down on the bench and put my head in my hands. She might still come. Anger clenches my insides. I have to get my car from her place. I get up and move toward the buses.

Eleven forty-six. I walk back to the bench and sit back down. Could her parents have found out and stopped her? This may not be her fault.

Twelve thirty-six. The homeless man gets half of a burger from a hurried passenger. He holds it out to me in silent offer, wiping his nose.

"Thank you, but you can have it."

He bites into the burger. Ketchup drips down his chin.

I stand up and head inside the station to the buses.

Three minutes past one. Curtains are pulled tight against the windows of Nisha's house. My car sits in the driveway where I left it, its white coat gleaming under the high sun.

Trying to ignore the feeling that I'm stealing my own car, I get in. The leather scalds the backs of my thighs. I turn the AC on to full blast, and drive away. I'm too tired to care. I want to sleep for weeks.

Amma's car is in the driveway. My car crunches into its spot. My stomach churns.

When I was little, Amma used to say that I brought the most happiness into her life. After losing a daughter, my birth was a miracle. They named me Lakshmi. Beauty. Wealth. A few months later my father got tenure, and somehow I got all the credit.

I walk up the steps to our front door. The blue door is bumpy where the paint dripped from the edges. I slide my key into the lock, and let myself in.

I'm named after a goddess whose husband sleeps in a cosmic ocean of milk. One legend says that gods and demons churned the milk together, hoping for immortality, but instead they turned the milk to poison.

Amma sits at the dining table, almost hidden behind a stack of dentistry journals, her laptop open in front of her, reading glasses on. She looks up at me when I come in and goes back to reading something in one of the journals she has propped open with a coffee cup.

I try to summon up that numbness, to spread it through me and help me walk up the stairs to my room where I can sleep. I want to fall to the floor, fall through the floorboards and be swallowed up. I can't make the numbness come. I drag my legs to the dining table and sit down.

Amma ignores me and keeps reading. The skin under her bloodshot eyes hangs dark.

I sit and trace a deep groove in the pine table. Amma and Appa bought it when they first moved in and it amassed a collection of nicks and scratches over the years. Amma covers it when people come over.

I run the edge of my fingernail in the groove, around the crescent shape of it. I don't remember who made it, but it looks like the mark of a knife. I scratch at it, up and down and around, the wood digging under my nail.

When Lakshmi's husband incarnated as the human prince Rama, she became the avatar Sita, the most beautiful woman in the world. A good wife follows her husband. Sita was captured by a demon, imprisoned for years, and finally rescued after a great war. But now her chastity was in question. Rama ordered her to walk through fire to prove her purity. She didn't burn.

Amma shuts the laptop with a thud. She takes off her reading glasses and stretches her hands in front of her. She leans her elbow on her laptop and pinches the bridge of her nose. "It's not easy, Lucky," she says. "After your father left, I worked hard to be part of this community. I paid a lot for my mistakes. I don't want you to suffer like I did."

I make my voice as soothing as I can. "I won't suffer, Amma."

"Of course you will." She spits out the words. "You don't know how hard it'll be until you don't have it. Our world isn't kind to women without husbands."

I'm not part of this world she's afraid of, this community she clings to, these uncles and aunties who compare each other's kids like pieces of fine jewelry. These people don't belong to me. The words sound harsh even in my head. They get caught on my tongue. I dig my nail into the knife mark, up and down and around.

"Don't play with your life, Lucky. You can't be happy living like these Americans."

She acknowledges the possibility, and rejects it. *Can't.* I get up from the table.

"You're going to destroy the reputation of this family," she says.

I walk upstairs to my bedroom, and close the door on Amma's voice.

Even after Sita proved her fidelity, questions remained in the minds of the people. Rama, now king, sent his pregnant wife into exile because he couldn't stand the shame. She raised her kids alone in the woods, and when they were grown, she called upon the earth to swallow her up, and it did.

⁓

Grandmother's coughs scrape themselves out of her throat and fall around her. I bring her glasses and glasses of water during the day, place another by her bed at night, and wake up to go help her drink it. She stays in the folding chair all day, and when she gets tired of that, she stares out the sliding glass doors. Sometimes I take her to sit on the deck to work out the pain in her knees. She leans heavily on me when I help her walk, favors her left leg, and throws her coughs behind her.

The heat outside refuses to let up, even with November creeping over us. The sunlight taps against our skins when we go outside. Even the floorboards of the deck soak up the warmth and radiate it back into our feet like asphalt.

Grandmother cups her hand behind her ear and listens. I catch a small wail in the air, but as soon as I hear it, it's gone, leaving only the sound of the air around us.

"The babies are dying." She stretches out her neck like a turtle into the breeze. "I can't hear them now." Her eyes are clear, the blue eating more and more of the brown from the outside in. Tears drip out and down her cheeks. "The babies are dying, Vidya. They want to be born."

I wipe away her tears with a kerchief. "There are no babies."

"I hear them, Vidya. They're dying."

I try to tell Amma. "She's getting worse," I say.

Amma pulls on her thick suede gardening gloves over blue latex ones that she took from work.

"She's getting worse," I say again.

She tightens the Velcro straps on her gloves. "I'll worry about Grandmother. You just worry about you. It's what you're good at." She opens the sliding glass doors and walks out onto the porch.

Grandmother snores on her folding chair in the living room.

I follow Amma. The air swirls with a slight chill but the sun prickles on my shoulders. Amma walks down the steps to her garden, still going strong in the unseasonal late-fall heat. The grass slides wet and cold under my bare feet.

She crouches down and starts to pull out the weeds that have crept in. "Now you're trying to convince me you care. How selfish."

My shadow swallows her.

"All you care about is going out and drinking with your friends," she says.

The sun is starting to singe through my pores. I think of numbness. I need to hold onto that feeling.

"What did I do to deserve daughters like this?" She stops weeding and sits back into the grass.

Imagine me without my weight. I'd just float off the earth, my bones growing hollow like a bird's.

"I've tried to tell you, Lucky, but you don't listen to anyone. You're going to end up alone."

She presses her face into her dirty gloves. I crouch down and try to pry her fingers away. She resists. She cries and pulls at her hair, heaving sobs down into her soiled gloves.

"Amma." I try again to wrestle her hands away.

The gloves leave dirty streaks down her face. "You think it's my fault that Vidya ran away?"

I open my mouth but the answer won't come. It's not your fault. Grandmother isn't my fault. Blame solves nothing. But I can't wrap my tongue around the lies.

She pushes me away and kneels down next to her garden. "It's my fault, right? My fault. Everything's my fault." She pulls at a healthy pepper plant, rips it out, and tosses it into a pile of weeds. "I'm a terrible mother." She pulls another plant hanging low with eggplants, and tosses it into the weeds. "I'm a terrible wife." Pulls and pulls out one plant after another.

I grab her shoulders and try to push her back but she's heavier and shakes me off. I fall backward into the grass.

She grabs the last onion plant and shakes it at me. "Go," she says. Loose dirt falls from the exposed roots. "Get away from your terrible mother. It's what you want, isn't it?"

I scramble to my feet.

"Just go." She hits her chest with her fists again and again. "Go."

I should stay. I should stay. I turn and run, away from her, away from the bald garden and the pile of healthy dead plants.

I go to the rugby house and tell Tasha what happened. We sit and smoke on the deck. The wind is back to normal—cool but not yet cold—carrying with it red and yellow leaves, slowly stripping the trees in the neighborhood. Tasha nudges me and points toward a car that is parallel parking. A small blue Honda. Nisha's car.

"Do you want me to go inside?" Tasha asks.

"No." I put my hand on her knee. "Stay."

We watch Nisha pull in behind a Smart Car and get out. She looks at us, but I can't see her expression.

She walks up to the house. I take my hand from Tasha's knee.

Nisha climbs up the creaky steps and stands in front of us. I stare at the peeling strips of paint on the wood floor.

She digs around in her purse and pushes something at me. A

gold envelope that glitters in the sun. I take it slowly and open it. She holds out another one for Tasha.

The wedding invitation is cut in the shape of a woman's facial profile. Milky skin and a long, aquiline nose, head draped in a red saree that opens to reveal text printed in gold. Tamil on one side, English on the other.

Tasha holds the card close to her face and looks at the Tamil script she can't read.

"I want you to come," Nisha says.

"I'll come."

She pulls out another invitation from her purse and drops it through the mail slot in the front door.

Tasha holds out the one Nisha gave her. "You can take this back."

"You're not coming?"

"I'm coming with Lucky. I'm her date." Tasha shakes the invitation at Nisha.

Nisha's face twitches and for a minute I think she's going to cry. But then she takes the gold envelope and puts it carefully back into her purse, turns around and walks to her car. The wind blows her long hair into her face. I want to call her back, stop her, shake the sense into her.

"I hope you don't mind," Tasha says as Nisha drives away. "That I said I was your date, I mean."

"You can't make it any worse."

She puts her hand on my knee and traces circles into my jeans. "The tournament's getting close. We need a place to practice properly."

I turn Nisha's wedding invitation around and around in my hand. The glitter sheds onto my skin. I can't scratch it off. I think of Nisha's dark hair, splayed out on her bed, in the back-seat of her car, on the mats of our old high school.

"I know of a place," I say.

⁓

That night I take Tasha, Jesse and two other girls to Winchester, through the side door of the high school that I know they keep unlocked for the theatre kids who practice late. We sneak through the long E wing, up to the gym, up again to the darkened wrestling room, navigating with the light from our phone screens.

The smell of sweat cooks in the heat of the room. We pull off our shoes and crawl on the mats to find each other in the dark. Jesse sets up a flashlight in the corner. She and another girl pull on their gloves and helmets and face off first while Tasha and I find seats against the wall.

"Are you all right?" Tasha asks.

I press my back against the mat and slide down onto the floor. "Fine."

Jesse and the girl circle each other.

Tasha's fists beat a soft rhythm against the floor mat. "That was really fucked up what Nisha did. The wedding invite and everything. You can't tell me you're okay with all that."

The smell from the mats is overpowering.

"I know it's not my business. But she's hurting you. I wish I could help."

"I'm fine." I scrape the mat with my knuckles.

Jesse blocks a kick and dodges a punch.

"She shouldn't be stringing you along."

"Shouldn't you practice what you preach?"

"I don't string people along."

"You don't commit to them, either."

Jesse grabs the girl's forearms and powers her to the ground. She knocks out Jesse's knee with a kick. Jesse falls down heavily. She grabs the girl's shoulders and pushes her flat to the floor.

"You're a beast," the girl says.

Jesse helps her stand and they both strip off their gloves. They shake hands.

Jesse comes over and offers me her gloves. I push my fingers into them and she straps me in. She takes her helmet off and secures it on my head. My short, prickly hair sticks out through the holes of the padded helmet.

Tasha gives me a fresh mouth guard and I put it in. She's already padded and ready. We face each other. Tasha bounces back and forth. I keep my distance.

She feigns a punch. I step back. The mouth guard slides around. I bite down on the soft plastic.

She lunges at me again. I take another step back.

"Don't let her corner you," Jesse shouts from the side.

I'd have to take my eyes off of Tasha to check how much space I have behind me. Step to the side, circle around. But Tasha's in the way. She comes closer. I keep my hands up to shield my face.

She comes close enough to make contact. I step back, feel the wall against my back foot. Nowhere to run.

"You have to go for it," Jesse says. "Punch her."

I try to visualize the energy flowing from my shoulders, try to twist with my waist but Tasha's eyes glow in the dim light and I can't do it.

"Punch me," she says through her mouth guard. She steps in closer and aims a jab to the side of my face. The glove makes contact with my forearm.

I instinctively punch back. My glove lands on her shoulder.

A phone vibrates in the room. I feel it through the mats.

"It's for you, Lucky. It's your mom."

Tasha aims a punch to my shoulder. I can't dodge in time. My skin stings with the impact.

"How's it feel?" she says.

The panic rises, that jitteriness in my fingers, my knees. Cornered.

"Just push through," Jesse says. "Don't close your eyes."

Tasha lightly touches my glove with hers. "Push me back."

I keep my eyes open. Step forward. Feign jabs. She steps into the middle of the room. We circle each other. The mats vibrate with a phone call.

"It's your mom again."

"Shouldn't you get that?"

"No." I can't talk well around the mouth guard.

Tasha's hands fall slightly from her face. "Maybe she wants to make up."

I feign a punch. She puts her fists up. How much would a punch to the gut hurt? Don't think too much. Act with the body. Trust the body. It knows how to survive.

I punch, twisting from the gut. For a split second I forget I'm punching another human being and it feels too easy until Tasha folds at the point of contact and sways toward me. I catch her, lift her upright. "I'm sorry."

She coughs a laugh. The mats vibrate with Amma's call.

"I can keep going." She pulls herself up and punches me in the stomach.

Air rushes out of my lungs. Vertigo.

I punch back, blindly. My gloves make contact again and again.

Her hits twist me. My insides hum. My brain rings. I feel lighter with each hit.

Another punch and she sways toward me. I hold her. She puts her gloved hands on the sides of my head and presses her forehead to mine. Her hair is cold. Our noses slip against each other.

"Forget about Nisha," she says.

The floor vibrates with Amma's call. Four calls.

I close my eyes and think about the space between my face and Tasha's.

Amma calls again. Five.

I step away from her. Jesse takes off my glove so I can call Amma.

Appa picks up the phone. "It's Grandmother. You need to come home."

⌒

I don't speak to Tasha as she drives me to the hospital. It's an effort to even say goodbye, to thank her for driving.

I don't speak to Appa or Laila Aunty when I find them in the waiting room. They don't speak to me. Laila Aunty looks like she's going to come hug me, but Appa holds her back by the hand.

I walk into a room decorated like a hotel, nothing like the

sterile rooms she's been in before. Grandmother lies under a mound of blankets and tubes. The light's been turned down. There's a window that shows the stars rising outside.

Amma sits in an armchair by the bed. I stand by her shoulder.

She strokes Grandmother's hand with one finger and doesn't look up. "She asked for you."

Grandmother lies still, the blankets around her unmoving.

"She asked for you," Amma says again. Her voice cracks.

Something drops in the very middle of my insides. Grandmother lies still and cold. The last bits of sunlight hang frozen in the air.

Silence eats through the house. Five ugly bruises form on my face and arms. Amma doesn't notice. My face aches every time I move it, but inside I'm hollow. Inside, I can't feel a thing.

Appa comes to see us almost every day, usually with a container or two of Laila Aunty's curries. We sit around with tea, watching the news on TV. Democrats take the Senate. A divided nation reelects Obama.

Grandmother's folded chair leans against the glass sliding doors that lead to the deck.

When I can't take the silence, I go upstairs to Grandmother's room and lie on her bed, finding patterns in the popcorn ceiling. Some of Vidya's drawings are still taped to the walls of my old bedroom, each one carefully preserved in a plastic sheet protector and stuck on with tape. She drew me whatever I asked for, and I spent hours trying to copy her loose-wristed sketches. I send her one last email, telling her what happened.

The sheets smell like Grandmother's skin, like the soap she liked to use. I hate the smell, too strong and flowery, but in the mornings I wash my face with it anyway. I can't let it sit there, unused and softening in a plastic dish in the bathroom, its mint green blending in with the walls.

I could've gone home to Kris, could've never come to this house again. I could've walked away.

Vidya's drawings watch me. She drew portraits of Amma, Shyama, me, Nisha. Appa's portraits are missing, just empty spaces, holes in the crowded wall. Interspaced among us are pictures of Matt Damon at various ages and Wonder Woman in reimagined costumes that made sense. The small metal sculpture, her senior year art project, stands where it always did, a miniature of the orange metal outside of her apartment in Louisville.

Amma and Appa plan the funeral. I want to help, to do something besides lie on Grandmother's bed in the new November heat, but I can't. I lie crushed into the blanket. I'm useless. Have I always been so useless?

Tasha wants to come and see me, but I tell her not to. I can't upset Amma more. I step around her like a shadow. She sits in the living room and watches the election coverage for hours on end. She goes to work even though she's eligible for bereavement leave. I wish I had work to go to, something to structure my life. At night when she isn't watching the news, Amma sits with her laptop and dentistry journals, her reading glasses on the tip of her nose. I sit with my laptop, trying to work on commissions I've neglected. I finish the pixie drawing, and the man who ordered it threatens not to pay unless I lighten the pixie's skin. I lighten her skin. He pays me enough for a month's mortgage on our Bridgeport house. I draw two portraits of couples for wedding invites, a battle scene of a young mage against a blurry medieval army, and a painting of John Watson kissing Sherlock on a bridge in the rain.

Amma and I don't talk. What would we say? We sit with the lights off, our faces lit by blue screens, private and alone in our grief.

People come by our house to pay their condolences. Laila Aunty has cooked everything. Rice and curries line up in aluminum trays on the dining table. People swirl around the house. I stay close to Kris and no one tries to talk to me. Amma sits on the couch and cries. Shyama and Laila Aunty sit beside her. I want to console her, to hold her as she cries, but I can't make myself push into the grief circling around them.

Grandmother looks more lifelike than before she died. Her face drips over whatever they've pumped through her to keep the flesh firm. Only around the edges of her fingernails can I see the gray striations of a decaying corpse.

Perfume wafts from the coffin, flowers and chemicals and something sweet. What sort of death smell is it trying to cover?

They dressed her in her favorite saree—dark green with embroidered white squares, a flower garland and a gold chain around her neck. There's a sharpness to her white hair that I don't understand. It's so crisp now, like each strand reflects the light differently.

Amma sinks at the knees, grips the edges of the coffin for support. I hold her around the waist and prop her up. Shyama stands watching Grandmother's feet. Amma's sister-in-law couldn't get a visa in time to come from Sri Lanka. It's just the three of us—our small family even smaller in the viewing room.

I wonder if Grandmother's eyes are completely blue now, if the clear ring around them has taken over the burgundy. I wonder if her gums are still stained with betel leaf.

Grandmother once told me about Hindu funerals. Loved ones shrieking, women rocking backward and forward, their unclipped hair keeping time with their movement. But this is New England, a white funeral home, and my mother swallows our traditions for theirs. She cries quietly, doesn't let the grief swell out of her and settle over the room.

They give us a half hour with Grandmother in the small room that seems to close in on us, then take the coffin to the main viewing room for the wake.

An obscene blue sky shines through the windows. I sit at the front with Amma on one side and Shyama on the other. Kris and Rajesh sit behind us and pass little Varun back and forth between them.

A man I don't know sings nasal Hindu prayers into a microphone without taking a breath. His raspy crooning soaks into the walls. Thick carpet muffles footsteps and people seem to appear out of the sunlight, kissing me on the cheek and holding Amma while she heaves quietly. There are people I haven't seen since my own wedding, or even since I was little. Amma's friends, family friends who took Appa's side in the divorce, Amma's co-workers. Maybe I should have invited Tasha and Jesse to the wake. Maybe it would've been the polite thing to do.

Death has washed us of color—everyone wears white and black and brown. No adornments, no jewelry.

"She lived a full life," they say. "It was a peaceful death." No one comments on my buzzed hair, or the bruises on my face showing through my concealer.

Flower wreaths line the wall, propped up on metal stands, each with a banner declaring who sent them. There's one that says, "From Lakshmi, beloved granddaughter." I've never seen it before.

Nisha and her parents, all dressed in dull, worn gray, stand at the end of the line. Nisha has her hair up. She walks close to her parents like they're all encased by the same invisible cage. They make their way to the coffin.

Kris taps me on the shoulder. "Are you okay?"

My head is too full to nod.

Nisha's parents walk toward Amma. Nisha's eyes slide over me, refusing to look, landing instead on Grandmother in her coffin.

Her parents murmur to Amma, who clasps their hands. Nisha walks to the coffin. She looks down into it, her ponytail fanning across her back.

Kris taps my shoulder again. "Go talk to her."

I dry my palms on my thighs and stand up.

Amma sniffs and wipes at her eyes. Nisha's parents are distracted.

I walk quietly to Nisha and stand behind her. "I fought with Tasha."

She turns around. "Why?" She doesn't have her contacts in, and I love the darkness of her eyes.

I run my hands over my hair, feeling the bristles slide under the pressure of my palm. "It was just for fun." I show her the bruise on my arm that I haven't covered with makeup.

She presses a finger into the darkened skin.

Grandmother lies still in her coffin. Amma said she asked for me. Not the me she thought was Vidya, or the me she thought was a boy. She asked for Lucky, the me she remembered.

Nisha steps closer and tucks her chin down. Little bits of water hang on her eyelashes. With a look toward her parents, she whispers, "They won't let me leave the house. They won't let me leave."

My head is too light. Blood floats in me, up and up like it's going to float away. "Do you want me to come get you?" That's what happens in Tamil movies. The heroine is forced into a marriage but her lover arrives at the last minute and carries her off. The bride belongs to the man who brings her home.

Nisha looks at her feet. "I don't want to get married."

"You can back out."

"It's too late." She shuffles her feet closer to mine. The tips of her ballet flats touch the toes of my oxfords. "I'm sorry about Grandmother."

I nod at our feet. We slouch toward each other. She takes my hand and rubs my palm with her thumb. My blood wants to float away, to twist out of my skin and fuse with the air.

Nisha pushes my bangs to the side. I sink and she catches me. For the first time she feels solid against me, like she can hold me up. She rubs her wet cheek against mine. Grandmother asked for me. All she wanted was to see Vidya, hold a baby.

Someone pulls me away from Nisha. I stumble.

Nisha's mother's face squeezes into the space between us. She leans toward me and whispers in Tamil, "Don't you touch my daughter."

I put my hands up and step back.

She jabs her finger into my sternum.

"Don't," Nisha says weakly.

Her mother whirls around. "You need to be a good girl."

Shyama walks up next to me. "Please, this is a funeral."

Appa and Laila Aunty appear on either side of me.

Nisha's mother looks around at us. "You should all be ashamed." Sunlight pinches her face in shadow.

Amma pushes her way into the circle. "You need to go."

"Do you know what your daughter did?"

"You need to go."

Nisha's hair swipes back and forth across her back as her mother grabs her by the arm and drags her away.

Amma clutches her chest. Laila Aunty catches her before she falls. Shyama goes to them and puts her hands around Amma. The three of them stand there, holding each other up. A wail rises in chorus, wrung out of the air. The sound pulls at my skin. I walk toward them. Amma's arms press against my face. Their wail surrounds me, crests over me. I hold onto Amma's shoulders.

The funeral ceremony is moderated by a priest who looks like the one from my wedding. A distant male cousin comes from Toronto to do the last rites for Grandmother because Hindus believe that women, givers of life, shouldn't be the ones to send life passage from this world. His bare shoulders slope forward as he follows the priest's instructions, repeating chants and prayers in a low rumble I can't make out.

Teenagers hold incense by the coffin. I stand with Amma and Shyama and watch Grandmother. The smoke washes over my face, into my chest.

Grief is an impossible meal, so we cut it up into little pieces, dress it in ritual, and take it like a pill.

When the funeral-home workers come to close the coffin, Amma drapes herself over Grandmother. Shyama and I pull her off. We walk with the coffin and the mourners to the crematorium, a procession of black and white under the clear autumn sky. Someone throws flowers that crush under my feet.

Normally women don't go to the cremation, but when the funeral-home workers say they'll allow six people into the room, Amma puts a hand on the back of my neck and guides me in.

Grandmother's coffin sits on a conveyor belt. The priest says the last chant, then tells us to push a button.

Amma ushers me forward, and I press the button that sends Grandmother through a set of black curtains. She should've burned on a funeral pyre of wood and cow chips, the flames and wild night dancing around her, but instead she melts quietly inside a box.

Two days after the funeral, after Shyama and Kris go home,
I get an email from Vidya. *Meet me at the Winchester
library at 2. By the pond. Today.* No mention of Grandmother,
or the funeral. At Vidya's words, I seize up and sit there at the
computer, unmoving for a hundred long days. I make up an
excuse for Amma, say that I'm going to go get a book to read,
that I need it to fill the time and the awful silence in my head.
She tells me to get one for her, too. Something happy, she says.
A happy story.

I arrive at the library early, and spend my time looking for
a book for Amma. My hands shake between the shelves. My
mind runs through my fingers. I can't hold a thought. I walk
out empty-handed. Still early. I walk around the pond. A thin
film of ice rests on the water. I play the scene over and over in
my head. I would say, "Why didn't you come for the funeral?

Grandmother asked for you. Amma misses you. Come home. Come see her." What I imagine is a turnabout of the memory in which Vidya and Amma fight. A reversal. This time, Vidya would apologize. Amma would melt.

Vidya sees me before I see her. I finally catch sight of her as I'm rounding the corner. She's waving from the back door of the library. Her daughter is holding her hand. The girl chews on her fingernail and stares up at me. She's older than in the photo I have, but not by much. There's a pinprick in my sternum. I don't realize the changes in Vidya until I get closer. She's darker, her skin leathery like too much sun and not enough sunscreen. Her hair as short as mine used to be. The wrap of her coat shows a waist thinner than I remember. A crazy thought passes through me, and I wonder if she's sick.

"Look at your hair," Vidya says.

She hugs me. She smells unfamiliar, like peonies and something else I can't place. She rubs a hand over my head.

"You look great," she says, and sounds like she means it. "This is Radha." She kneels next to her daughter, points up at me. "Radha, this is your Lucky Chithy."

The girl smiles shyly at her own feet. I can tell she'll look like Vidya someday, like Grandmother in the picture where I thought she was a princess.

"She's brought something for you," Vidya says. "Go on."

Radha digs in a mirrored purple purse and draws out a bag full of clacking shells. She holds it out to me.

"These are shells from all the beaches we've been to," Radha says. I want to believe she even sounds like Vidya, but I can't remember what Vidya's voice used to be at four years old.

"She's been collecting them for years," Vidya says.

I take the bag from Radha. The shells are multicolored, some minuscule, some as big as my palm.

"Are you sure?" I ask. "I don't want to take away your collection."

"They're just things," the girl says. "I don't need things."

Vidya kisses the girl on the forehead. Radha follows us while we walk around the pond. I think of all my questions. There are too many, cluttering up my mouth.

"I've been following your artwork online," she says before I can speak. "You've gotten quite good."

"It pays the bills. Why did you put that address on your letter?"

"I don't remember which address I put." Her voice is light, almost uncaring. "I like your art."

"Kentucky. Louisville. I went looking for you."

She puts a hand on my shoulder. "I didn't think you'd do that. I haven't lived there in years."

"Where do you live then?"

"Everywhere."

She tells me that she's been traveling around the country with her daughter for two years in a minivan, driving coast-to-coast, teaching classes on papermaking.

"It's not so bad, Lucky. I'm free."

"Free from what?"

"Expectations." She stops to watch a young boy eating alone on a bench, ripping off bits of his sandwich and feeding it to the ducks. "I don't like being told what to do."

I gently touch the shells in the bag. Their stripes, their curves.

"Grandmother always talked about you," I say. I watch to

see if she'll cry, but she seems smoothed out and serene like the iced-over pond.

"I'm sorry about Grandmother," she says. "I know you must miss her."

"Don't you miss her?"

Her smile is free of pain. "I miss all of you."

I form the question in my head but she answers before I can ask.

"I can't come home, Lucky."

"Amma misses you."

"I can't come home. Maybe someday."

"But—"

"Amma's love comes with strings, Lucky. You know that better than anyone. I can't deal with strings. I like my life. I have Radha. I'm happy." She looks at me with pity. The longer I look at her, the less she resembles the sister I remember. "You deserve to be happy, too. I hope you know that."

"I'm happy." I say it without thinking, an automatic response.

She turns away. "I don't want to pry. I don't presume to know your relationship with Kris, or your sexuality."

"Then don't. I could be bisexual."

"Are you?"

I briefly consider lying.

"Are you?" she says again.

"No." Nisha's face looms behind my eyelids. Her wedding in less than a week. "Come home. Amma would be so happy if you came home."

She doesn't consider it for even a second. "I made my choice, Lucky. I like my choice. I'm not going to muddy it up now."

"But you're all alone." I imagine leaving, getting in my car and driving until I can't drive any more. Picking a place on a map, making a new home. Could I leave Amma all alone? She has no one else now. Or maybe she'll bend. She has no one else now. Could she learn to live with the real me?

"And anyway," Vidya says, "I love traveling. We get to go all over the country. Wake up in a new place every week."

"What about Radha?"

"Radha loves it. She's learning papermaking, and she gets to make friends at every place we go."

"But shouldn't she meet her family? Her grandmother?"

Radha pulls on my coat. She's wearing a flowered skirt over blue pants. I'd been too distracted to notice earlier. She shows me a book she pulls out from her purple bag. It's an Atlas, and she flips to a map of the US. She tells me where she got each shell. Haulover Beach. Block Island. Saint George Island. San Luis Obispo.

"They're mementos," she says, stumbling over the word.

Vidya starts walking again, and Radha trots behind us, still looking at the map. "I wanted her to meet you," Vidya says. "I wanted to make sure you're okay. You were Grandmother's favorite."

I don't know why this is the thing that makes me cry, but it does. Vidya hugs me to her.

"I was young, Lucky," she says into my shoulder. "I made my choices and I didn't think enough of you. I'm sorry."

"Come back, then. Come back and see Amma."

She wipes my face with her scarf and puts her hands on the sides of my face like she used to do when we were younger.

"I only came to see you, Lucky. I left Amma behind a long time ago."

In less than an hour they're gone, Vidya claiming she has to be in Vermont before nightfall to speak at an artist's studio about letterpress. I walk around and around and around the pond alone, learning the shape of each shell.

Nisha's wedding day.

Nisha's wedding day and it snows, white shedding from the sky and floating in the air. The house turns cold. I can see my breath when I wake up.

Nisha's wedding day and I haven't decided what to do. Indecision sits in my chest, something sharp when I breathe.

According to Hindu rites of mourning, I'm not allowed to go to a wedding until a month after the funeral. I wake up, brew coffee and mix oatmeal for Amma. When I go back to my room, my bed's already made and Amma has laid out a saree for me. The blue of it cuts through my eyes. I've gotten used to the colors of death: the pale creams, charcoal grays, inky blacks.

"I can't go," I say.

Amma holds herself up by the wrought iron headboard, thick rings under her eyes, her face sunken in and dusty. "Nisha is your best friend." Even her voice is dusty. I've forgotten what it sounds like. "You should go."

"But the rules—"

"—can be bent just this once. She wants you there. Go."

I dress myself while Amma waits outside the door. Once around and tuck. Pleat and tuck. Twice around, pin.

I paint my face, watching the layers go on one over the other in the mirror. Battle armor of powder and sequins. Amma has no idea what she's dressing me for. Silence is the rule. Words are complications, sharp edges that cut up our tongues. We keep them in with walls of teeth, preserve the peace. Om shanti shanti shanti, as the prayer goes. Peace at any cost, as the prayer goes.

—

The Sheraton hotel wedding hall is dusted with snow. I shiver in my thin saree and join the trickle of people going inside. A cave of plush filigree carpet and fake candle lighting. A Ganesh statue welcomes me. Sweet almonds, here have some more, take a lassi.

I could throw open the wooden doors of the wedding hall, stride up to the altar, offer my hand to Nisha. I could lead her out to my car in front of five hundred guests, take her home, run away to Toronto.

I wish I'd thought to tuck my flask into my saree.

I could push up Nisha's wedding saree, remind her what she's chosen to give up, and leave her to her fate. I could go home to Kris and file for divorce.

I sneak past the guests to the elevator. Nisha said she'd be in room 407. I haven't told her that I'm coming. Will she be surprised? Will she have a bag packed?

Room 407. Nisha's wedding day. Silence behind the door. I knock.

Nisha opens the door. Makeup frames her bloodshot eyes. Her red mouth hangs open.

"I'm scared," she says. She doesn't move to let me inside.

I push past her into the room.

The door shuts with a metallic click. Snowlight floods through the window and over the room, lighting every edge a cold, clear white. Like Grandmother's hospital room.

"It's my fault," I say into the air.

"What?"

The rain. The soaked housecoat. The wheezing cough. The tubes. Pneumonia.

"Grandmother. It was my fault."

Nisha's arms wind around me. I want to melt at the knees.

Instead I say, "You look beautiful."

She presses her nose against my neck and cries. Her arms pull me closer, flush against herself, tighter, tighter until I want to push them away. Through the window, birds fly away in droves, finally leaving for winter.

Nisha quiets, sniffs away her tears. Her arms slide off me.

"They'll be back soon." She grabs tissues from a dressing table and presses them to the bottoms of her eyes. "Did you bring your car? Whose do we take?"

"You have your car here?"

She holds up her keys. "I drove."

"I thought they wouldn't let you leave?"

"They didn't."

"And yet you drove here."

She puts the keys back on the dressing table.

"Do you just need someone to do this with you?" I say. "Do you even care if it's me?"

She fiddles with the edge of her saree.

"Jesus, Nisha. No one has a gun to your head."

She holds out her hands and takes a step toward me. "What will I have if I leave this behind?"

The bride belongs to the man who—

"Do you want to go or not?" I widen my stance.

She looks at the floor and bites her teeth together. Walls of teeth. Keep in the things you want to say.

The bride belongs—

The room wavers. I walk toward the door.

The wedding has probably started. Both sets of parents will give their children away. Nisha's male cousin, stepping in for a brother, will guide Deepak to the flower-entombed altar. The priest will make a ring out of reeds and start the ceremony, his nasal chanting filling the room. When Deepak's sister comes to guide her to the altar, Nisha will stand up, grab the chair for support. Maybe she'll get used to the weight of the thali on her chest.

I stand in front of the door. "Are you coming?" I ask.

There's a saying in Tamil that a thousand lies can make a marriage. Here's the truth: I'm tired of lying.

Nisha is quiet, wrapping the loose end of her saree around and around her arm. I go back to her, draw her to me. I go to kiss her but she pulls away.

"We can have a life together," I say. "A real one."

She shakes her head. "I can't."

I try to catch her by the waist but she's walking away, toward the back of the room.

"I can't," she says. "I can't. You should go."

I make sure to leave the door open behind me. I half expect her to follow, but she doesn't.

In the wedding hall, she'll see Tasha sitting in the crowd as Deepak's sister guides her by the arm to the altar, drums beating a tune to her walk. Deepak will turn to her with the thali in his hand. The drums will beat louder and louder toward frenzy as he ties the thali around her neck like a noose.

I get back in the car. The windshield wipers push snow off the glass. I can't fight anymore. I can't save her. I said I would. It's the last lie I want to tell.

Amma is standing at the kitchen sink when I get home, watching the running faucet. Sound of pressurized water on steel. She startles when I touch her shoulder. I turn off the faucet and guide her to a chair.

"I'm getting a divorce," I say.

She looks up at me, her eyes struggling with understanding. Her face is puffy and ugly from crying. Her mouth mimes the word "no." No no no no no. She shakes her head.

I feel drunk, light-headed. I need air.

I open the sliding glass doors and walk out onto the deck. Grandmother's folding chair is still there, baking in the sunshine. I can't make myself sit on it, so I sit on the steps instead. Milky clouds stir over the sun, throwing shadows over fresh snow. Wind blows through my saree. Goosebumps, my feet curled with cold.

A high wail rides on the air, pierces through the light, the fog in my head. Like a baby crying.

I go back inside to where Amma sits. I touch her hand.

"Amma, come outside."

She looks up at me like she doesn't know who I am.

"Amma." I pull at her hand.

I lead her out of the house and into the sunshine.

"Listen." I close the sliding glass doors behind us. The hushed static of the house dies. "There's something crying."

Amma shivers, wraps her arms around herself. "I don't hear anything."

I pull her closer to the edge of the deck where I was sitting. "Listen."

She closes her eyes. Waits.

I hear it again, the high wail stretched thin.

Her lips open. She looks at me, then at our crumbling fence. "It's coming from somewhere." She walks down the steps to the backyard, barefoot in the snow.

I follow. We spread out, trying to follow the sound. Amma walks to the fence, drags her hand down one of the planks. I squat near her vegetable garden. She's replanted it, and the lettuce needs to be harvested before the snow melts. We'll be eating lettuce for weeks. The wail grows softer as I lean toward the garden. I head back toward the deck.

Amma trails her hand across the floorboards. I get down onto my knees in the cold snow and crawl forward. The deck floats about two feet from the ground, the underside of it dark and edged with rocks. I inch closer. Amma stops me with a hand on my back. Her hand clenches in my blouse, then slowly eases open, finger by finger.

I crawl under the deck toward the sound, using my phone to light the way. The smell of rot washes over me. My stomach turns. I pinch my nose and shine the phone screen in a wide arc.

Pressed up against the very back of the deck, a clumpy mass. Something moves.

I react without thinking. The phone slips out of my hand. I crawl back out and into the light.

Amma's face is still wet with tears, but she looks like she's forgotten to cry. "What's under there?"

"Something moved." My arms twitch. My legs want to run. "I dropped my phone."

She comes closer, reaches out and touches the bruise on my jaw, a mottled black starting to fade. "What happened to you?" Her eyebrows turn sad, and for a moment I think she's going to cry again. But all she does is turn my face this way and that and study the skin.

"Was it my fault?" she asks. "Did I make you like this?"

"It's not your fault."

She bends toward me, crumples at the waist and cries into the snow. "The community will hate you," she says. "They'll blame you for driving away a good man like Kris."

The snow is melting through my saree.

"Amma, Kris likes men. And I don't."

She shakes her head. "This isn't supposed to be your story. Not my daughter." She sounds more sad than angry.

I rub her arms, hold her to keep her warm. She keeps crying, coughing her sobs into the snow.

"This is what I want," I say. "I still have you."

The wail floats over our heads again. I wipe her face with the end of my saree. We crawl together, over the rocks and dirt until blackness surrounds us like film and the smell pours into our throats. I grab my phone and shine the light toward the back. What I thought was a clumpy mass is a pile of kittens, their fur matted and falling off their skin, their faces starting to peel back and reveal the bone underneath. Dead.

"Grandmother's babies," Amma says.

That movement again. That wail. One kitten still alive, small and dark and starved but alive. I reach out, cup it in the palm of my hand.

Amma and I wash the kitten in the sink, wrap it up in a blanket, and give it some milk in a saucer.

"I'll have to go to the store to buy cat food," she says. "Cow's milk is bad for them." She dips her finger in the milk and lets the kitten lick it off.

The kitten is already half-grown. Grandmother must have heard them when they were first born.

"You loved her," Amma says after a pause. "Nisha."

"I do."

There's pity in her eyes. "Maybe we should name this one Nisha," she says, petting the kitten.

"I wasn't kidding," I say. "I'm getting a divorce."

"But Nisha is married now."

"It's not about Nisha." I feel like Vidya, giving Amma one last chance before I become an empty chair. "I want to be me."

She stops stroking the kitten's fur. "Can you be happy like this? What would your life look like?"

Like an apartment in Cambridge, a job and a kitten and

midnight walks with a girlfriend. Like dancing at Machine with the rugby girls. Like short hair. Like looking in the mirror and never worrying about a stranger looking back.

Amma touches my bruise again, turns me toward the light. "We should put something on this." She rummages in the cabinets and takes out the sesame oil, a traditional remedy for scrapes and bumps. She dips a piece of paper towel in the oil and dabs it on my jaw. "Don't do this, Lucky," she says.

The kitten laps noisily at the milk. Amma covers my jaw in sesame oil, then cries. When I touch her arm, she says, "Leave me be. I've lost everyone." She backs away and up the stairs.

In every story there's what is written for you, and then there's what you write. I think of how to tell Kris. I think of Nisha in her wedding saree, walking up to her honeymoon suite in the hotel. I think of Grandmother sitting out on the deck, Vidya and her daughter collecting shells on the beach, Amma crying upstairs, mourning a story I never wanted to write. Can we escape fate? Can we change it?

My wedding photo laughs at me from the wall. I take the frame off its nail, slip out the print, and take it outside to the garden. Cold wind blows from the north. More snow coming, but after, the trees will bud and Amma will plant the garden anew. I dig with my hands and bury the picture deep in the earth.

ACKNOWLEDGMENTS

I'd like to say a heartfelt thanks to:

The friends who read the book in its early stages and gave me important feedback: Alex Vera, Amy Lamphere, Andy Lim, Bernice Olivas, Bethani Herring, Cole Papadopoulis, Daniel Nyikos, Evi Wusk, Jacquelyn Stolos, Jeff and Linda Bouvier, Jeffrey Schindler, Militza Jean-Felix, Mitchell Waters, Oliver Bendorf, Sammi Bray, Sarah Thomas-Dusing, Saretta Morgan, Susan Martens, and Todd Pernicek.

My professors and mentors at the University of Nebraska-Lincoln: Daryl Farmer, whose creative writing class made me put my ass in the chair; Timothy Schaffert, who first helped me believe that I could be a writer; Amelia Montes, who answered every panicky email and who listened, cared, and helped me through some of my hardest times; Starla Stensaas, who pushed me to follow my passion and opened my eyes to the concept that life is change and growth; Gerry Shapiro, RIP, who gave me some of the best writing and life advice I've ever gotten; Jonis Agee, who saw a novel in me and helped me start writing it; Judith Slater, whose kindness and care helped me figure out what I was trying to say; and Joy Castro, who tirelessly made sure I knew the right people in the right places at the right times.

Mark Winegardner, my major professor at Florida State University, and my professors Robert Olen Butler, Skip Horack, and Elizabeth Stuckey-French, for their support and advice about publication.

The New York State Summer Writers Institute and the Lambda Literary Writers Retreat for Emerging LGBTQ Voices, where I wrote great chunks of this novel.

The writers of Write Here Write Now, who accepted me when I was most broken and gave me a space to heal, with a special thank you to Toni Amato, who not only gave me meticulous feedback, but who also helped me believe that I'm capable of great things.

The friends who read multiple drafts, who listened to me rant for hours about my characters, and who have often been my own personal cheerleading squad: Annie Bierman, Jennifer Dean, and Ev Evnen.

Sam Majumder, for being my Kris. Scott Schneider for putting up with me and this project for as long as he could. And the writers and friends at Florida State University for celebrating art and weirdness with me these last few years, especially Jess

Cohen, Heather Bailey, Tom Tooley, Colleen Mayo, Gabby Bellot, Karen Tucker, and Rita Mookerjee.

My parents for giving me time and space to write, my brother Varun for being a walking anti-depressant, and Geoff Bouvier for being a wonderful muse, teammate, and life partner.

My agent, Connor Goldsmith, for believing in me and in the book, even when I didn't. My editor, Mark Doten, for seeing the book for the best that it could be and pushing me to get there. Rachel Kowal, Abby Koski, and all the folks at Soho Press for putting so much love and care into this book.

Y'all are wonderful humans. Thank you, thank you, thank you.